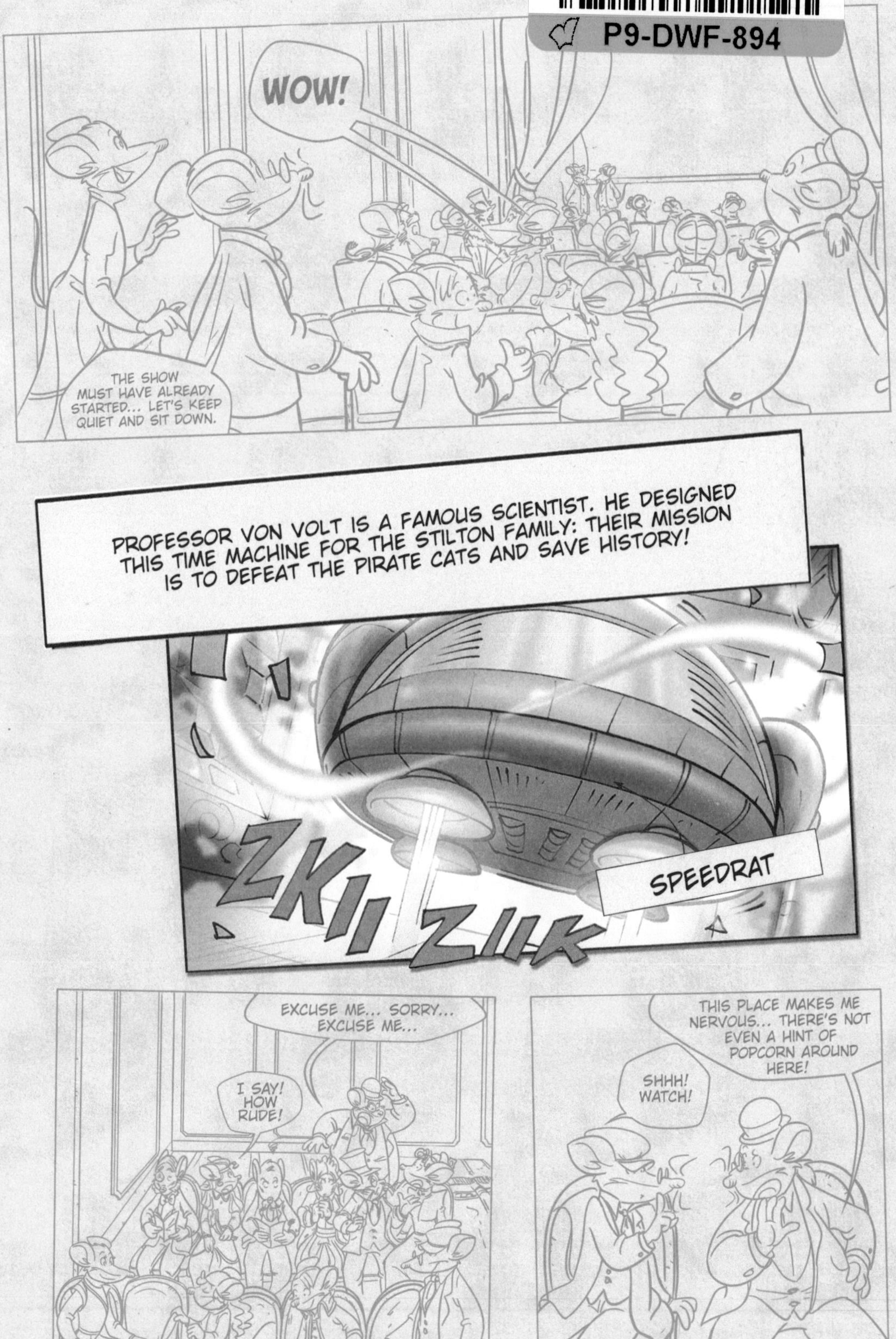
WOW!
THE SHOW MUST HAVE ALREADY STARTED... LET'S KEEP QUIET AND SIT DOWN.
PROFESSOR VON VOLT IS A FAMOUS SCIENTIST. HE DESIGNED THIS TIME MACHINE FOR THE STILTON FAMILY: THEIR MISSION IS TO DEFEAT THE PIRATE CATS AND SAVE HISTORY!
ZKII ZIIK
SPEEDRAT
EXCUSE ME... SORRY... EXCUSE ME...
I SAY! HOW RUDE!
THIS PLACE MAKES ME NERVOUS... THERE'S NOT EVEN A HINT OF POPCORN AROUND HERE!
SHHH! WATCH!

Geronimo Stilton

PAPERCUTZ™

Geronimo Stilton & Thea Stilton

GRAPHIC NOVELS AVAILABLE FROM PAPERCUTZ™
...ALSO AVAILABLE WHEREVER E-BOOKS ARE SOLD!

#1 "The Discovery of America"

#2 "The Secret of the Sphinx"

#3 "The Coliseum Con"

#4 "Following the Trail of Marco Polo"

#5 "The Great Ice Age"

#6 "Who Stole The Mona Lisa?"

#7 "Dinosaurs in Action"

#8 "Play It Again, Mozart!"

#9 "The Weird Book Machine"

#10 "Geronimo Stilton Saves the Olympics"

#11 "We'll Always Have Paris"

#12 "The First Samurai"

#13 "The Fastest Train in the West"

#14 "The First Mouse on the Moon"

#15 "All for Stilton, Stilton for All!"

#16 "Lights, Camera, Stilton!"

#1 "The Secret of Whale Island"

#2 "Revenge of the Lizard Club"

#3 "The Treasure of the Viking Ship"

#4 "Catching the Giant Wave"

papercutz.com

Geronimo Stilton

"LIGHTS, CAMERA, STILTON!

By Geronimo Stilton

PAPERCUTZ
NEW YORK

LIGHTS, CAMERA, STILTON!
© 2014 BAO Publishing
Graphics and Ilustrations © Atlantyca Entertainment S.p.A. 2014
Geronimo Stilton names, characters and related indicia are copyright, trademark, and exclusive
license of Atlantyca S.p.A.
All rights reserved.
The moral right of the author has been asserted.

Text by Geronimo Stilton
Story by Leonardo Favia and Francesco Savino
Script by Francesco Savino
Illustrations by Nicoletta Baldari
Color by Mirka Andolfo
Cover by Ennio Bufi and Mirka Andolfo
Based on an original idea by Elisabetta Dami

© 2015 – for this work in English language by Papercutz.
Original title: "Ciak, si gira, Geronimo Stilton!"

www.geronimostilton.com

Stilton is the name of a famous English cheese. It is a registered trademark of the Stilton Cheese
Makers' Association. For more information go to www.stiltoncheese.com

No part of this book may be stored, reproduced, or transmitted in any form or by any means,
electronic or mechanical, including photocopying, recording, or by any information storage
and retrieval system, without written permission from the copyright holder. FOR INFORMATION
PLEASE ADDRESS ATLANTYCA S.p.A.
Via Leopardi 8 20123 Milan Italy –foreignrights@atlantyca.it - www.atlantyca.com

Nanette McGuinness – Translation
Big Bird Zatryb – Lettering & Production
Jeff Whitman – Production Coordinator
Bethany Bryan – Associate Editor
Jim Salicrup
Editor-in-Chief

ISBN: 978-1-62991-208-0

Printed in China.
August 2015 by WKT Co. LTD.
3/F Phase 1 Leader Industrial Centre
188 Texaco Road, Tsuen Wan, N.T.
Hong Kong

Papercutz books may be purchased for business or promotional use. For information on bulk purchases
please contact Macmillan Corporate and Premium Sales Department at (800) 221-7945 x5442.

Distributed by Macmillan
First Papercutz Printing

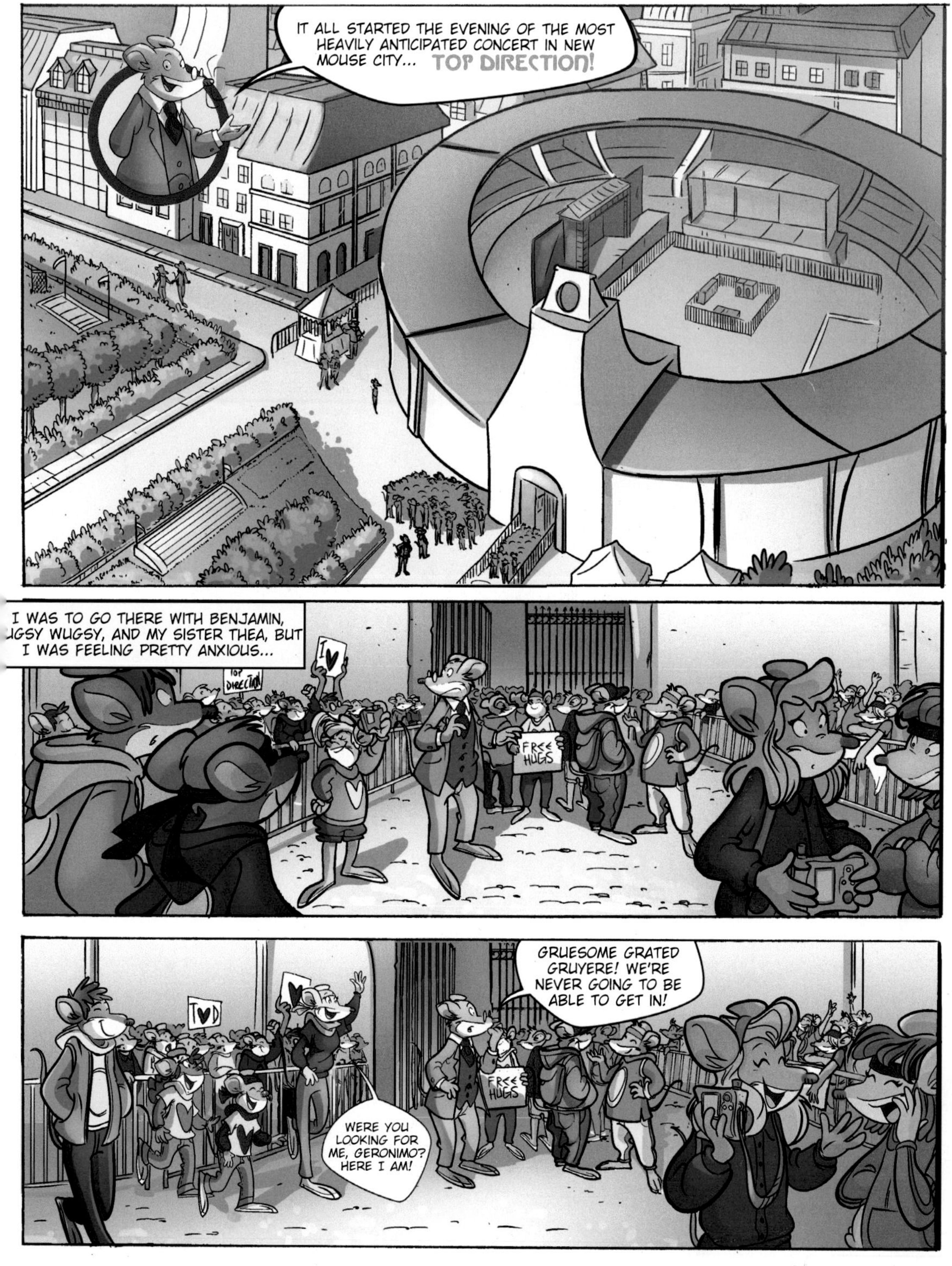
IT ALL STARTED THE EVENING OF THE MOST HEAVILY ANTICIPATED CONCERT IN NEW MOUSE CITY... TOP DIRECTION!
I WAS TO GO THERE WITH BENJAMIN, UGSY WUGSY, AND MY SISTER THEA, BUT I WAS FEELING PRETTY ANXIOUS...
TOP DIRECTION
FREE HUGS
GRUESOME GRATED GRUYERE! WE'RE NEVER GOING TO BE ABLE TO GET IN!
WERE YOU LOOKING FOR ME, GERONIMO? HERE I AM!
FREE HUGS

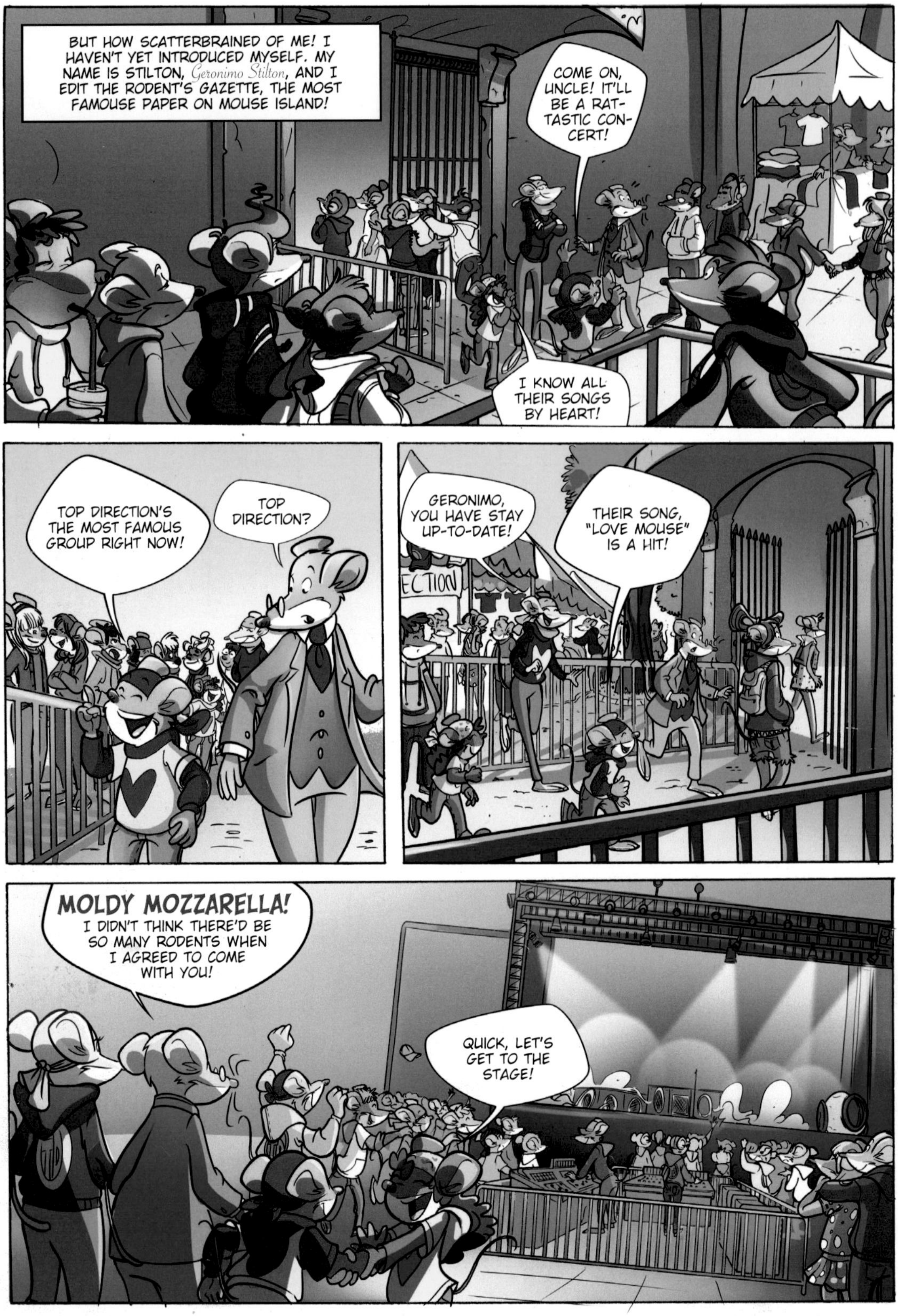
BUT HOW SCATTERBRAINED OF ME! I HAVEN'T YET INTRODUCED MYSELF. MY NAME IS STILTON, *Geronimo Stilton*, AND I EDIT THE RODENT'S GAZETTE, THE MOST FAMOUSE PAPER ON MOUSE ISLAND!
COME ON, UNCLE! IT'LL BE A RAT-TASTIC CONCERT!
I KNOW ALL THEIR SONGS BY HEART!
TOP DIRECTION'S THE MOST FAMOUS GROUP RIGHT NOW!
TOP DIRECTION?
GERONIMO, YOU HAVE STAY UP-TO-DATE!
THEIR SONG, "LOVE MOUSE" IS A HIT!
MOLDY MOZZARELLA! I DIDN'T THINK THERE'D BE SO MANY RODENTS WHEN I AGREED TO COME WITH YOU!
QUICK, LET'S GET TO THE STAGE!

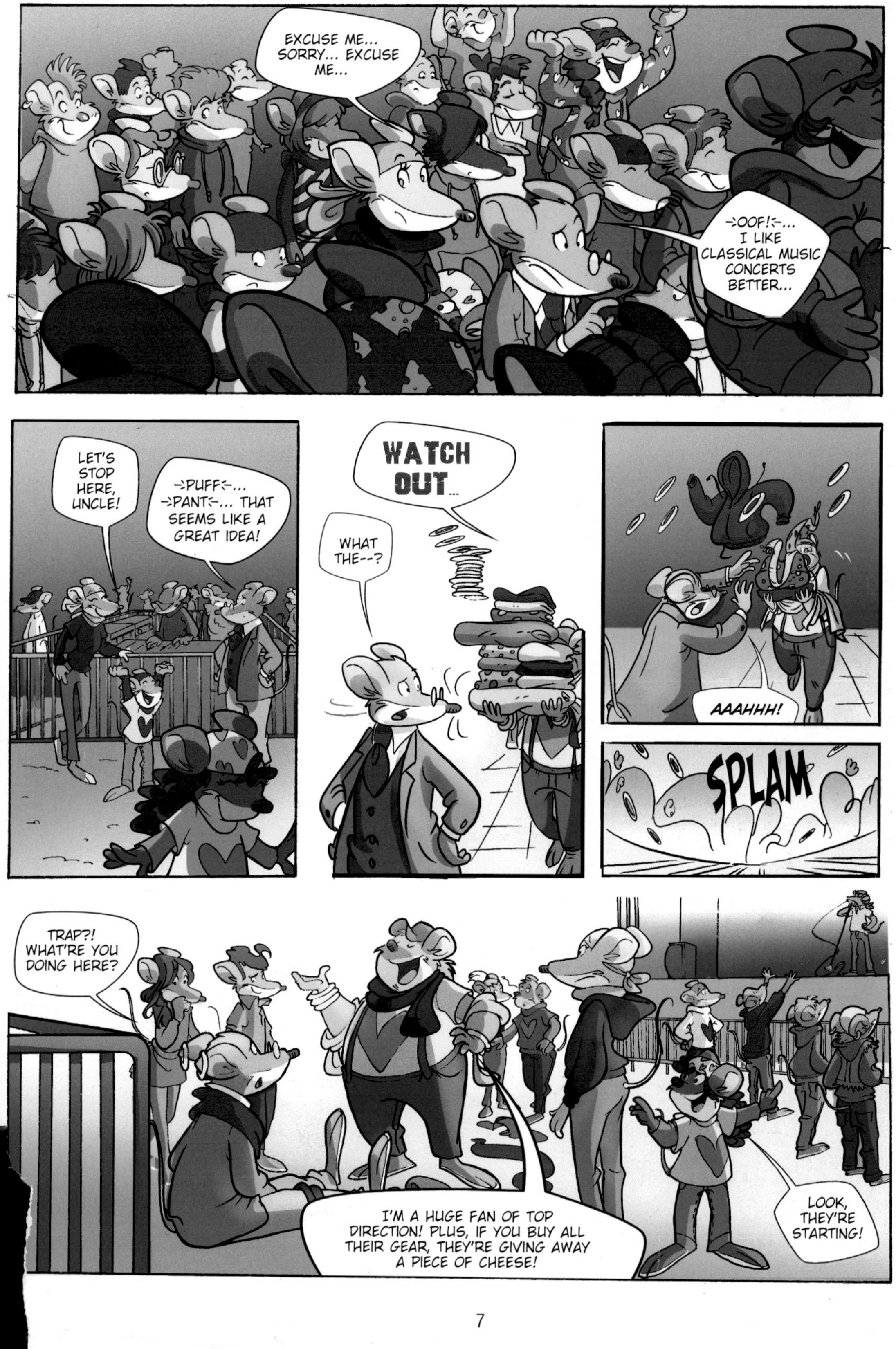
EXCUSE ME... SORRY... EXCUSE ME...
–OOF!–... I LIKE CLASSICAL MUSIC CONCERTS BETTER...
LET'S STOP HERE, UNCLE!
–PUFF–... –PANT–... THAT SEEMS LIKE A GREAT IDEA!
WATCH OUT...
WHAT THE--?
AAAHHH!
SPLAM
TRAP?! WHAT'RE YOU DOING HERE?
I'M A HUGE FAN OF TOP DIRECTION! PLUS, IF YOU BUY ALL THEIR GEAR, THEY'RE GIVING AWAY A PIECE OF CHEESE!
LOOK, THEY'RE STARTING!

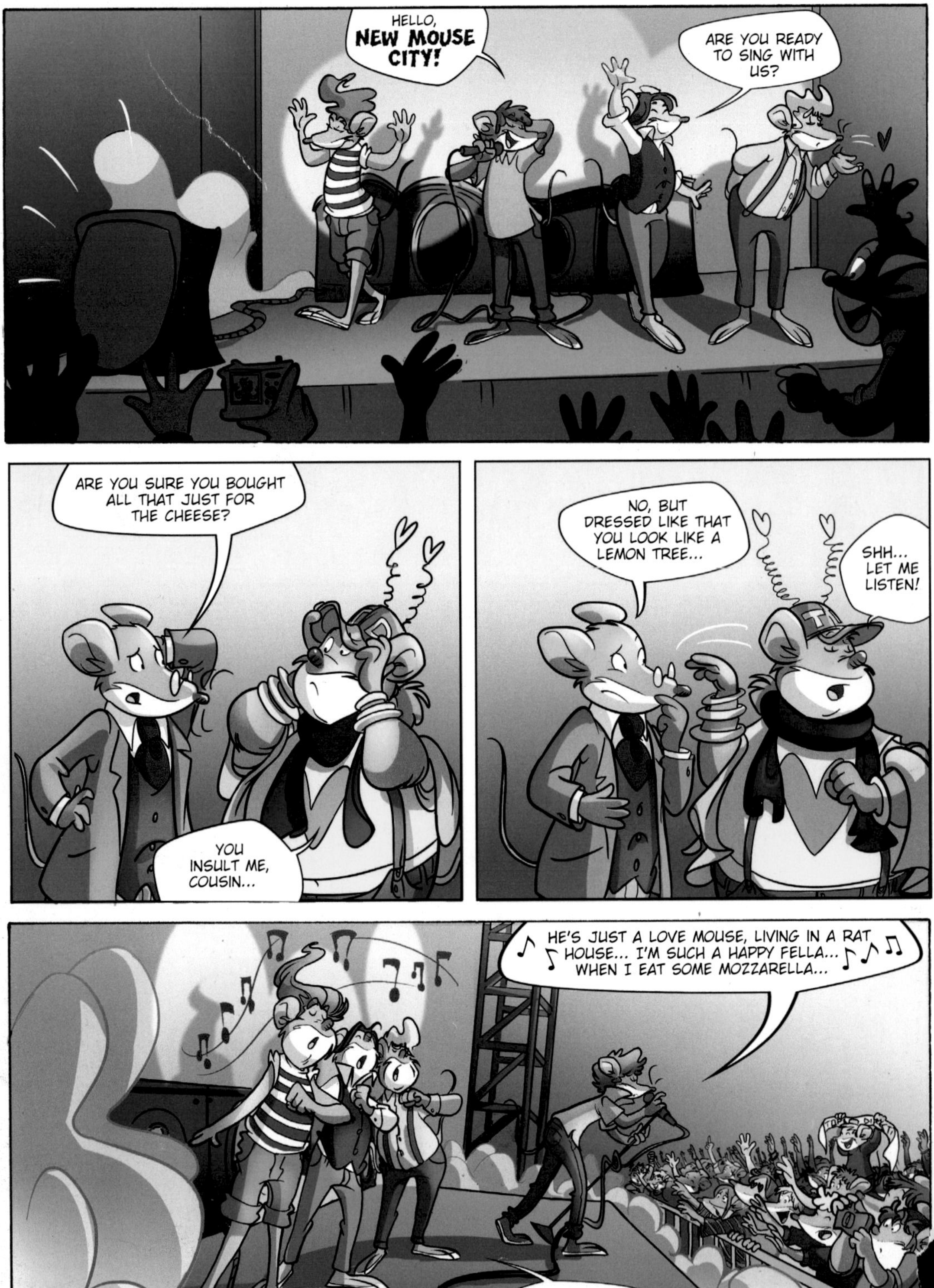
HELLO, NEW MOUSE CITY!
ARE YOU READY TO SING WITH US?
ARE YOU SURE YOU BOUGHT ALL THAT JUST FOR THE CHEESE?
YOU INSULT ME, COUSIN...
NO, BUT DRESSED LIKE THAT YOU LOOK LIKE A LEMON TREE...
SHH... LET ME LISTEN!
HE'S JUST A LOVE MOUSE, LIVING IN A RAT HOUSE... I'M SUCH A HAPPY FELLA... WHEN I EAT SOME MOZZARELLA...
mozzarella! mozzarella!

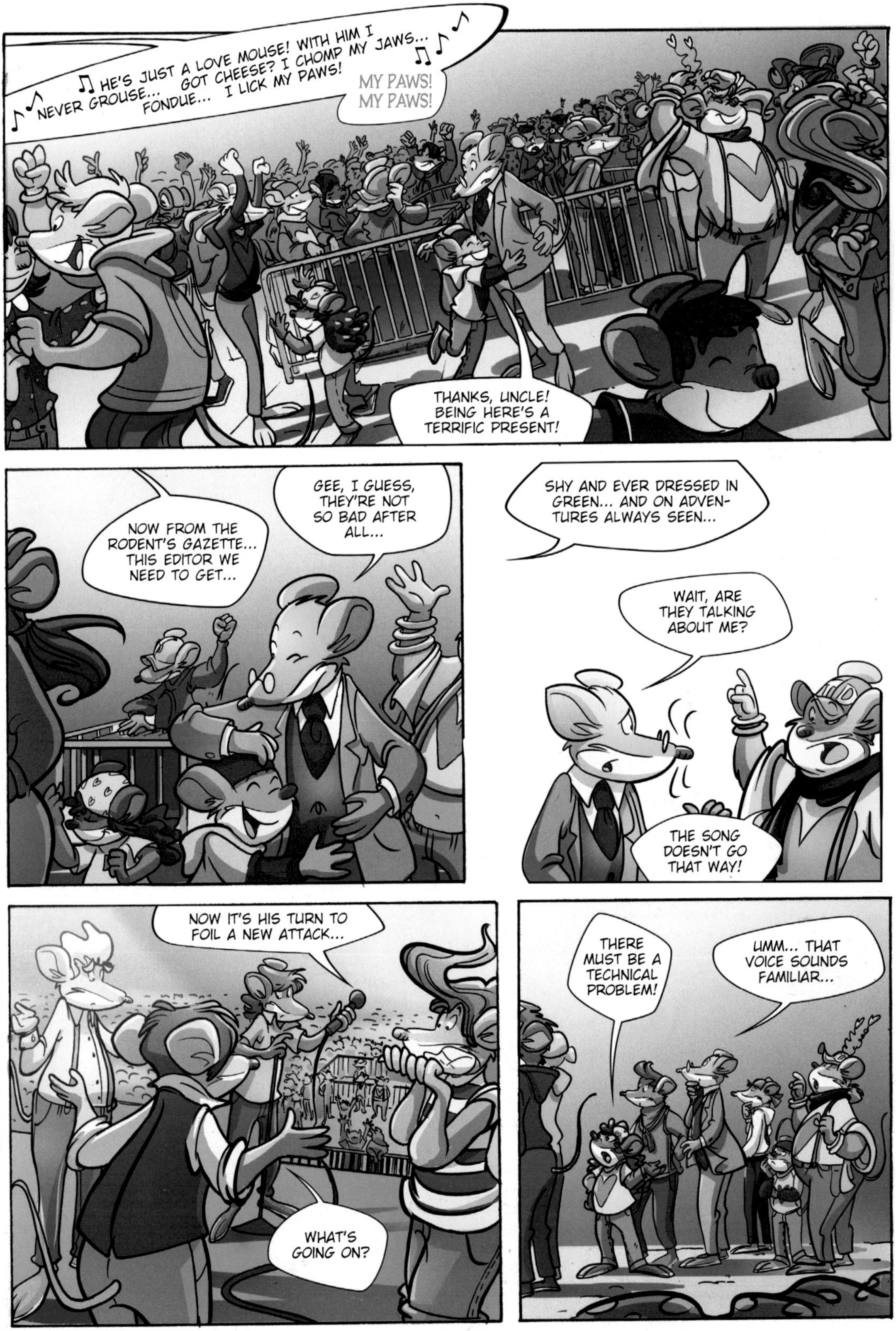
HE'S JUST A LOVE MOUSE! WITH HIM I NEVER GROUSE... GOT CHEESE? I CHOMP MY JAWS... FONDUE... I LICK MY PAWS!
MY PAWS! MY PAWS!
THANKS, UNCLE! BEING HERE'S A TERRIFIC PRESENT!
NOW FROM THE RODENT'S GAZETTE... THIS EDITOR WE NEED TO GET...
GEE, I GUESS, THEY'RE NOT SO BAD AFTER ALL...
SHY AND EVER DRESSED IN GREEN... AND ON ADVENTURES ALWAYS SEEN...
WAIT, ARE THEY TALKING ABOUT ME?
THE SONG DOESN'T GO THAT WAY!
NOW IT'S HIS TURN TO FOIL A NEW ATTACK...
WHAT'S GOING ON?
THERE MUST BE A TECHNICAL PROBLEM!
UMM... THAT VOICE SOUNDS FAMILIAR...

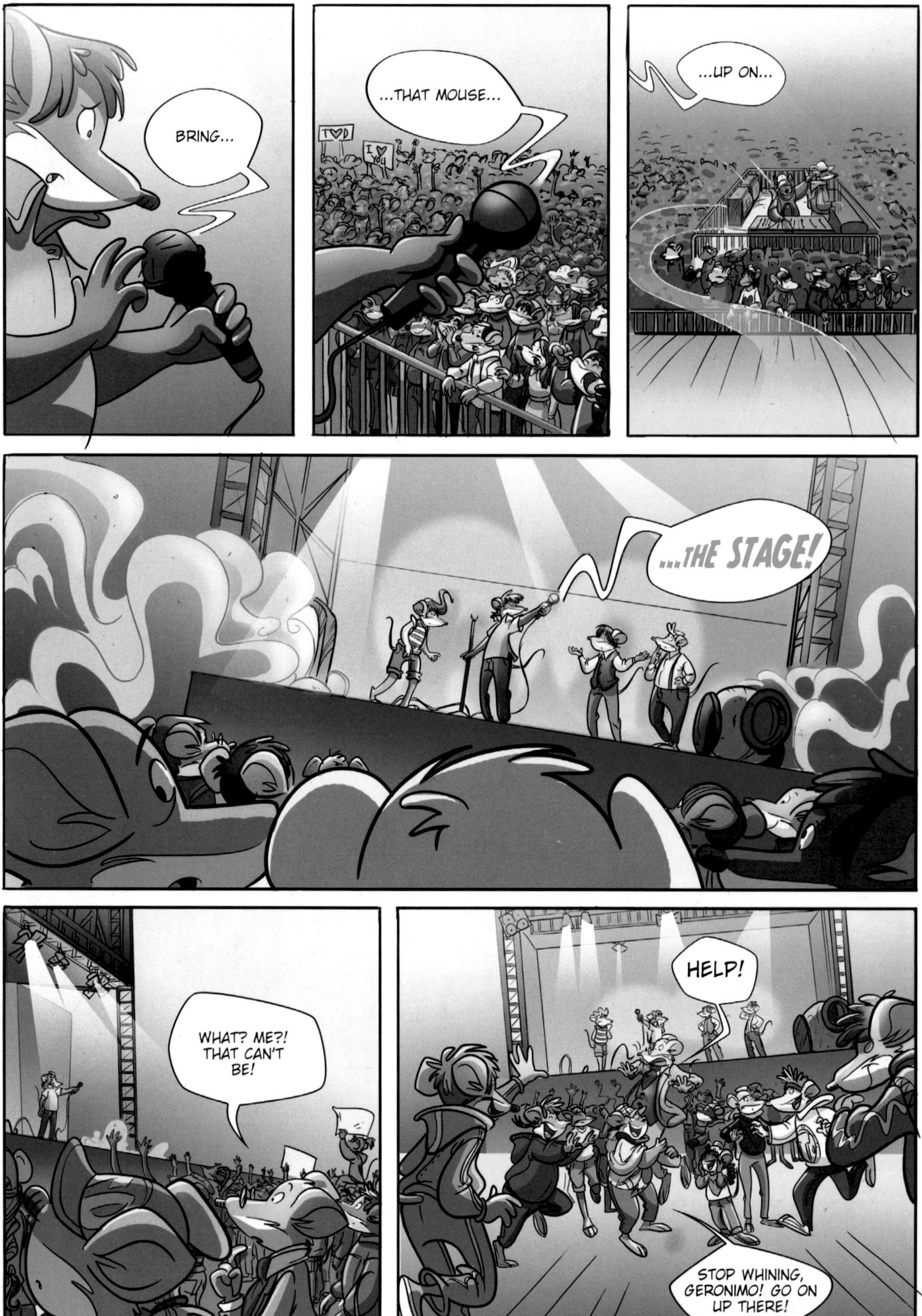
BRING...
...THAT MOUSE...
...UP ON...
...THE STAGE!
WHAT? ME?! THAT CAN'T BE!
HELP!
STOP WHINING, GERONIMO! GO ON UP THERE!

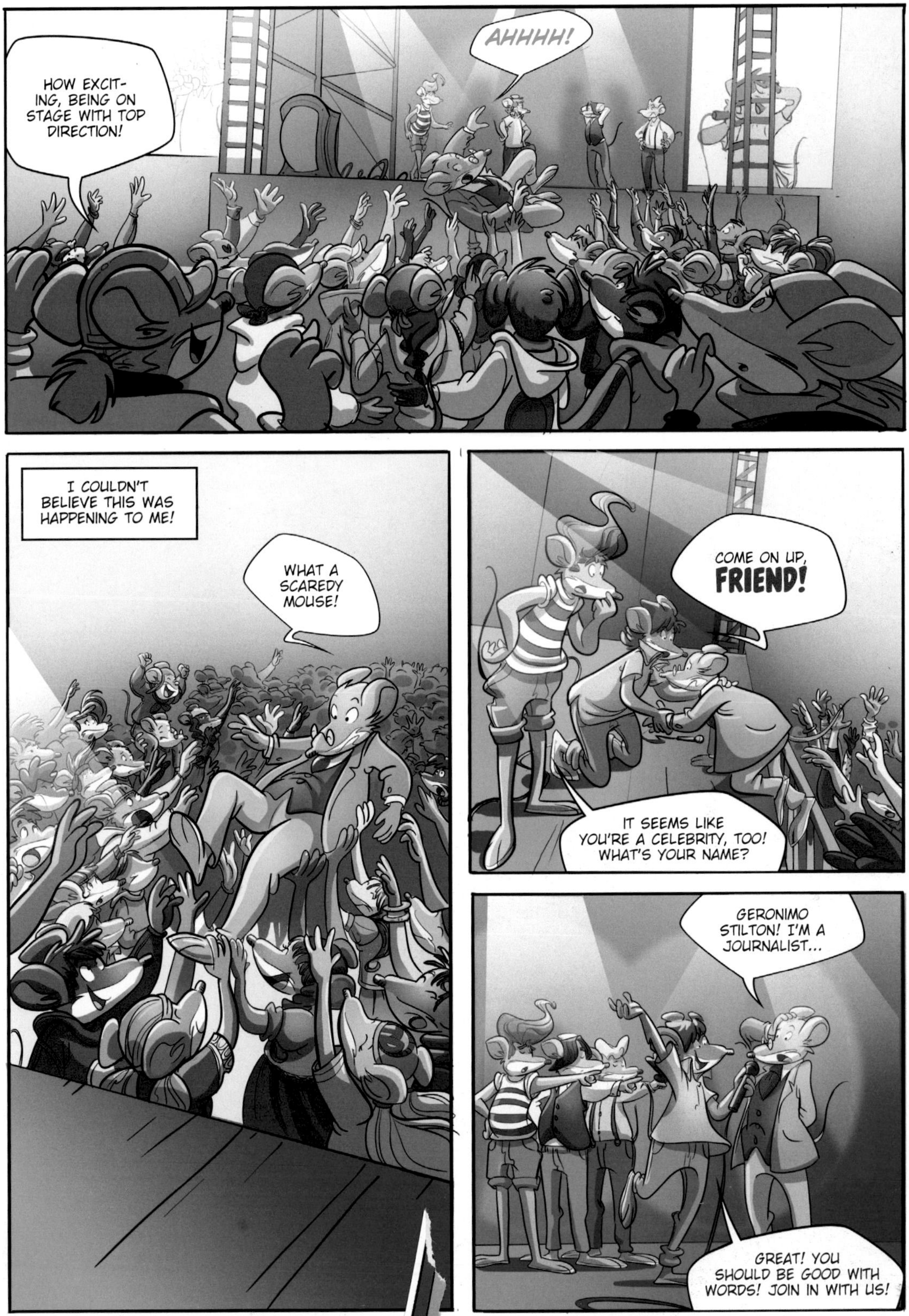
HOW EXCIT-ING, BEING ON STAGE WITH TOP DIRECTION!
AHHHH!
I COULDN'T BELIEVE THIS WAS HAPPENING TO ME!
WHAT A SCAREDY MOUSE!
COME ON UP, FRIEND!
IT SEEMS LIKE YOU'RE A CELEBRITY, TOO! WHAT'S YOUR NAME?
GERONIMO STILTON! I'M A JOURNALIST...
GREAT! YOU SHOULD BE GOOD WITH WORDS! JOIN IN WITH US!

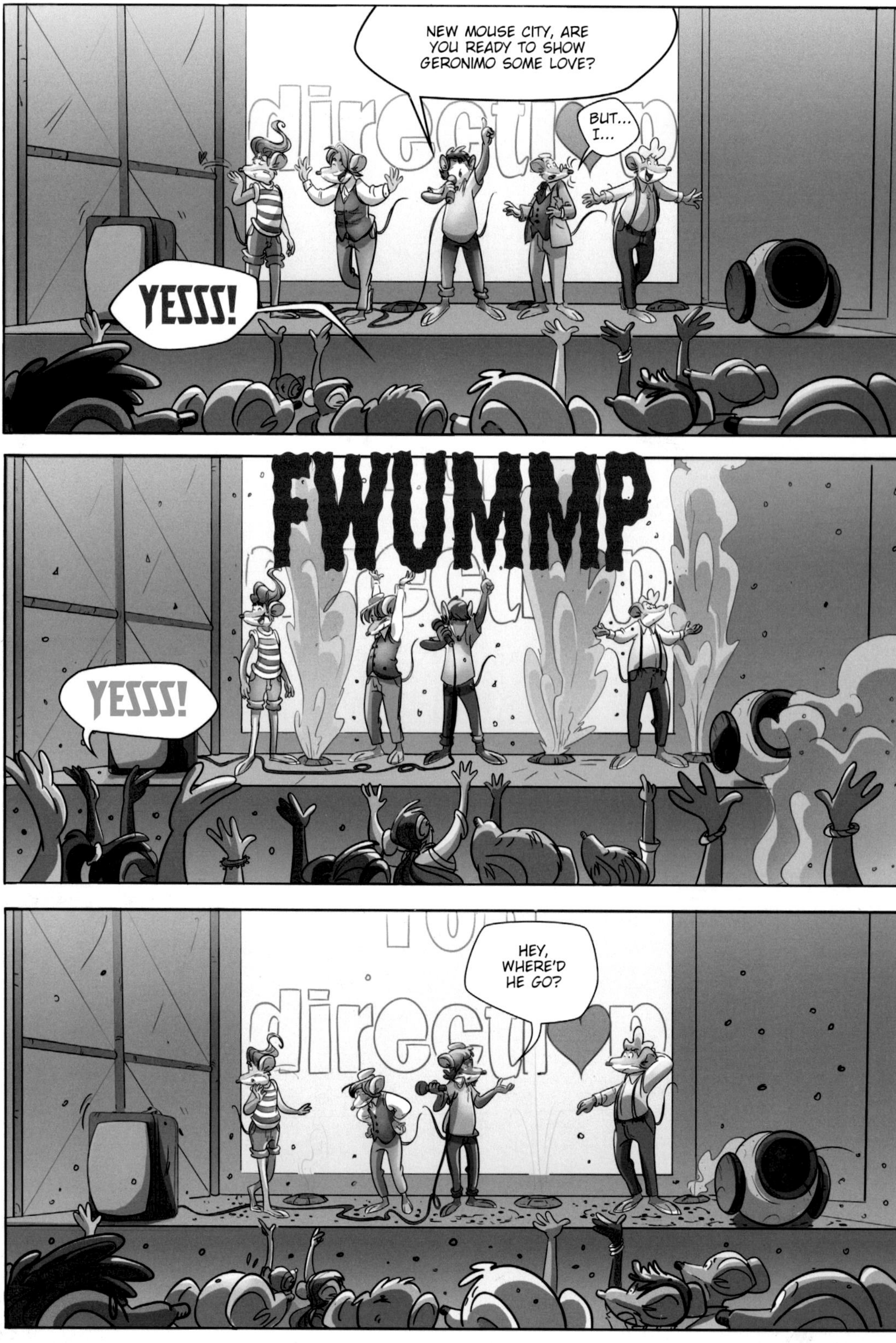
NEW MOUSE CITY, ARE YOU READY TO SHOW GERONIMO SOME LOVE?
BUT... I...
YESSS!
FWUMMP
YESSS!
HEY, WHERE'D HE GO?

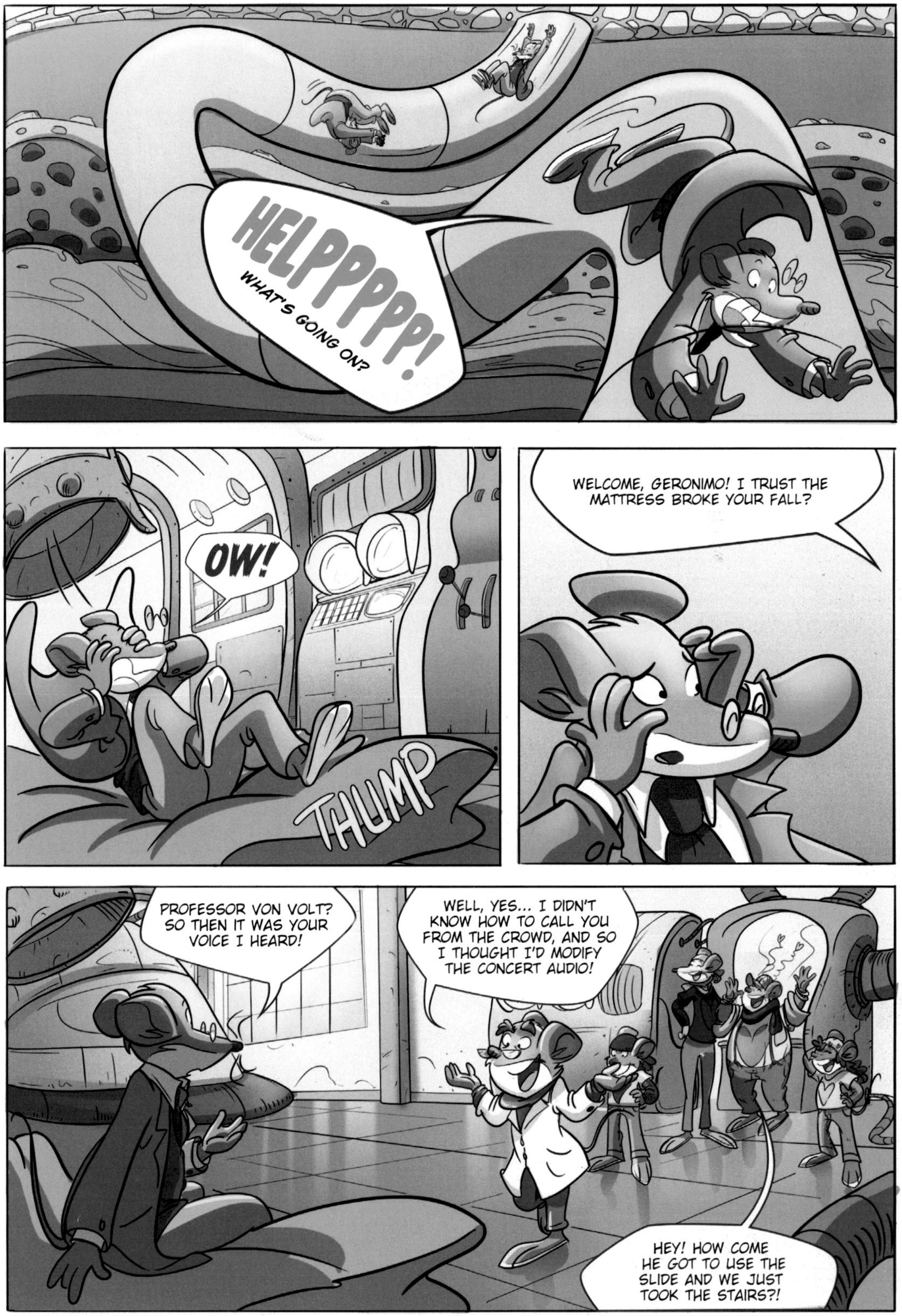
HELPPPPPP!
WHAT'S GOING ON?
OW!
THUMP
WELCOME, GERONIMO! I TRUST THE MATTRESS BROKE YOUR FALL?
PROFESSOR VON VOLT? SO THEN IT WAS YOUR VOICE I HEARD!
WELL, YES... I DIDN'T KNOW HOW TO CALL YOU FROM THE CROWD, AND SO I THOUGHT I'D MODIFY THE CONCERT AUDIO!
HEY! HOW COME HE GOT TO USE THE SLIDE AND WE JUST TOOK THE STAIRS?!

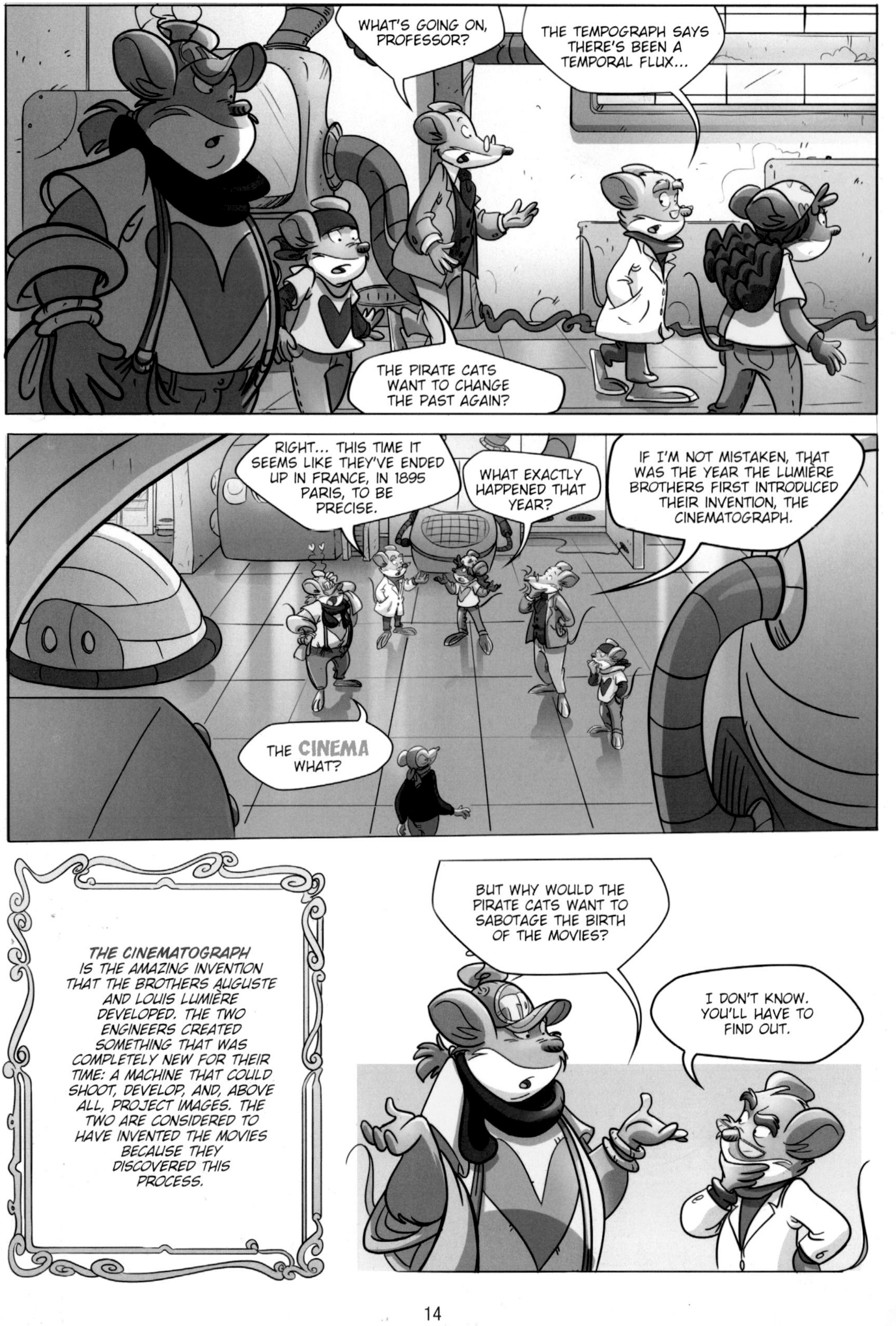
WHAT'S GOING ON, PROFESSOR?
THE TEMPOGRAPH SAYS THERE'S BEEN A TEMPORAL FLUX...
THE PIRATE CATS WANT TO CHANGE THE PAST AGAIN?
RIGHT... THIS TIME IT SEEMS LIKE THEY'VE ENDED UP IN FRANCE, IN 1895 PARIS, TO BE PRECISE.
WHAT EXACTLY HAPPENED THAT YEAR?
IF I'M NOT MISTAKEN, THAT WAS THE YEAR THE LUMIÈRE BROTHERS FIRST INTRODUCED THEIR INVENTION, THE CINEMATOGRAPH.
THE CINEMA WHAT?
THE CINEMATOGRAPH IS THE AMAZING INVENTION THAT THE BROTHERS AUGUSTE AND LOUIS LUMIÈRE DEVELOPED. THE TWO ENGINEERS CREATED SOMETHING THAT WAS COMPLETELY NEW FOR THEIR TIME: A MACHINE THAT COULD SHOOT, DEVELOP, AND, ABOVE ALL, PROJECT IMAGES. THE TWO ARE CONSIDERED TO HAVE INVENTED THE MOVIES BECAUSE THEY DISCOVERED THIS PROCESS.
BUT WHY WOULD THE PIRATE CATS WANT TO SABOTAGE THE BIRTH OF THE MOVIES?
I DON'T KNOW. YOU'LL HAVE TO FIND OUT.

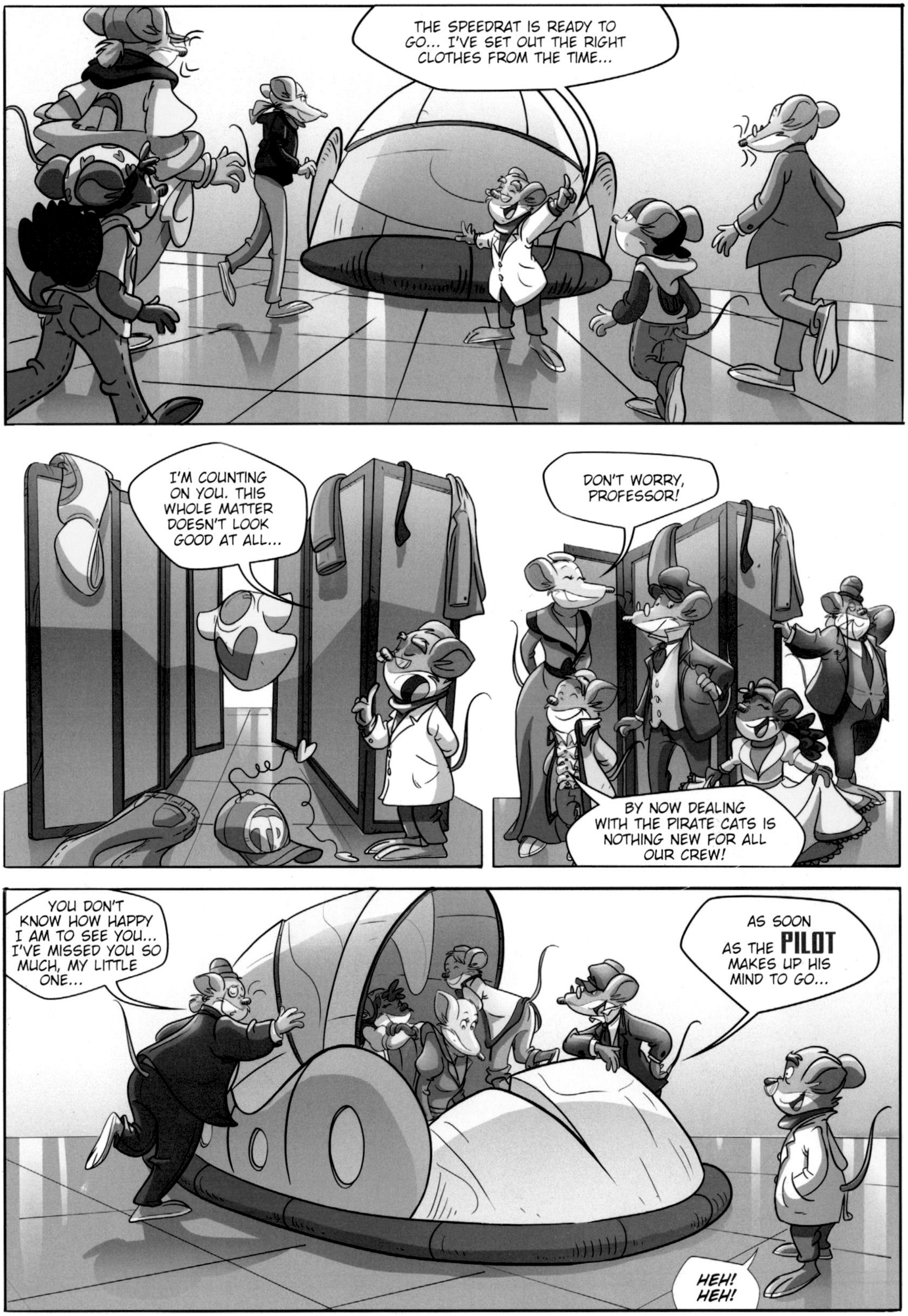
THE SPEEDRAT IS READY TO GO... I'VE SET OUT THE RIGHT CLOTHES FROM THE TIME...
I'M COUNTING ON YOU. THIS WHOLE MATTER DOESN'T LOOK GOOD AT ALL...
DON'T WORRY, PROFESSOR!
BY NOW DEALING WITH THE PIRATE CATS IS NOTHING NEW FOR ALL OUR CREW!
YOU DON'T KNOW HOW HAPPY I AM TO SEE YOU... I'VE MISSED YOU SO MUCH, MY LITTLE ONE...
AS SOON AS THE PILOT MAKES UP HIS MIND TO GO...
HEH! HEH!

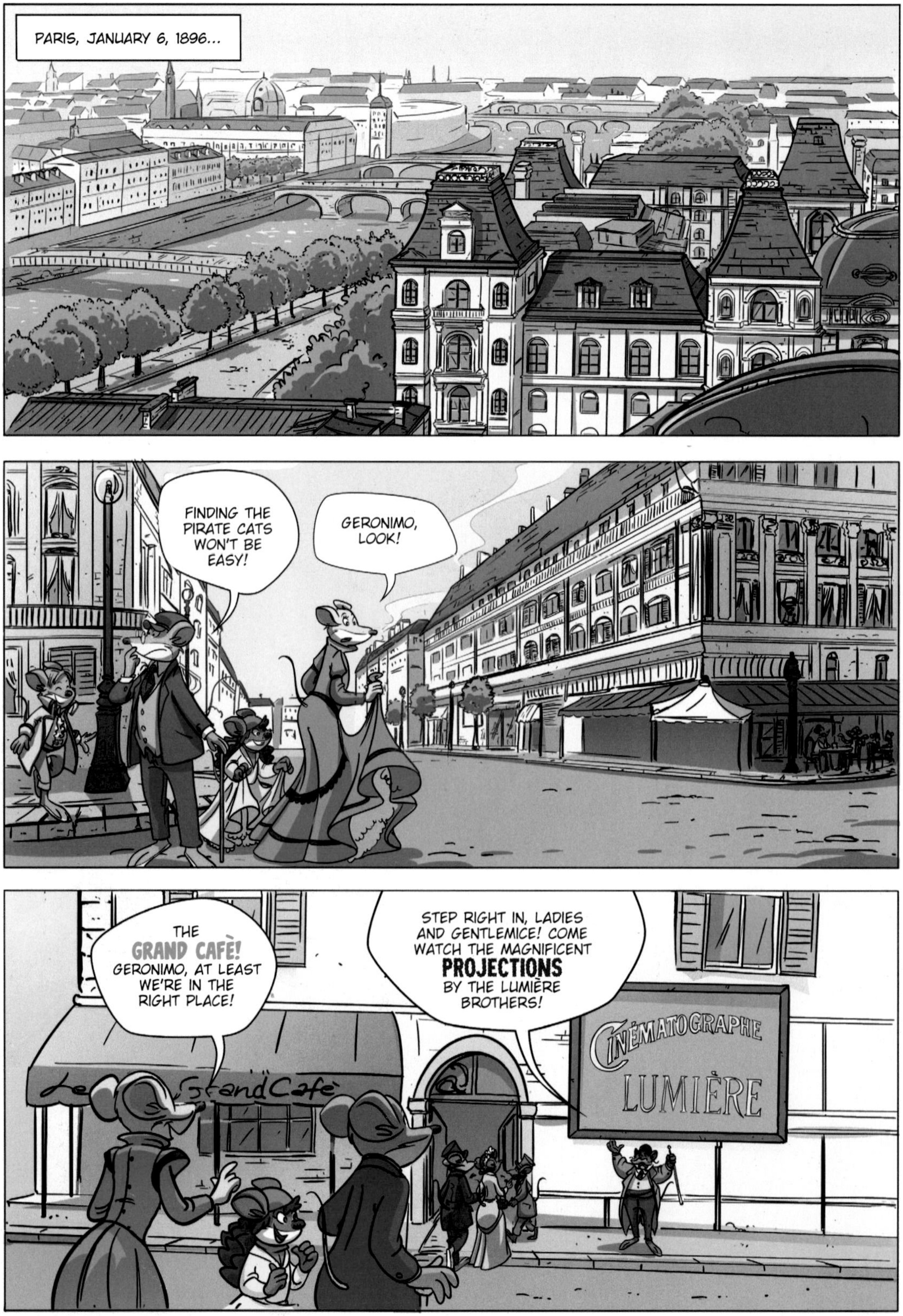

PARIS, JANUARY 6, 1896...
FINDING THE PIRATE CATS WON'T BE EASY!
GERONIMO, LOOK!
THE GRAND CAFÈ! GERONIMO, AT LEAST WE'RE IN THE RIGHT PLACE!
STEP RIGHT IN, LADIES AND GENTLEMICE! COME WATCH THE MAGNIFICENT PROJECTIONS BY THE LUMIÈRE BROTHERS!
Le Grand Cafè
CINÉMATOGRAPHE
LUMIÈRE

HMM... YOU'RE RIGHT. THE PIRATE CATS COULD BE HERE IF THEIR GOAL IS TO GET TO THE LUMIÈRES. WE'D BETTER GO SEE THE SHOW!

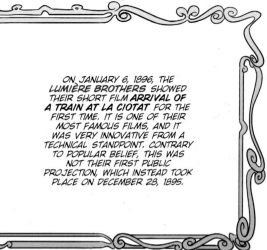

ON JANUARY 6, 1896, THE **LUMIÈRE BROTHERS** SHOWED THEIR SHORT FILM **ARRIVAL OF A TRAIN AT LA CIOTAT** FOR THE FIRST TIME. IT IS ONE OF THEIR MOST FAMOUS FILMS, AND IT WAS VERY INNOVATIVE FROM A TECHNICAL STANDPOINT. CONTRARY TO POPULAR BELIEF, THIS WAS NOT THEIR FIRST PUBLIC PROJECTION, WHICH INSTEAD TOOK PLACE ON DECEMBER 28, 1895.

WOW!

THE SHOW MUST HAVE ALREADY STARTED... LET'S KEEP QUIET AND SIT DOWN.

EXCUSE ME... SORRY... EXCUSE ME...

I SAY! HOW RUDE!

THIS PLACE MAKES ME NERVOUS... THERE'S NOT EVEN A HINT OF POPCORN AROUND HERE!

→SHHH!← WATCH!

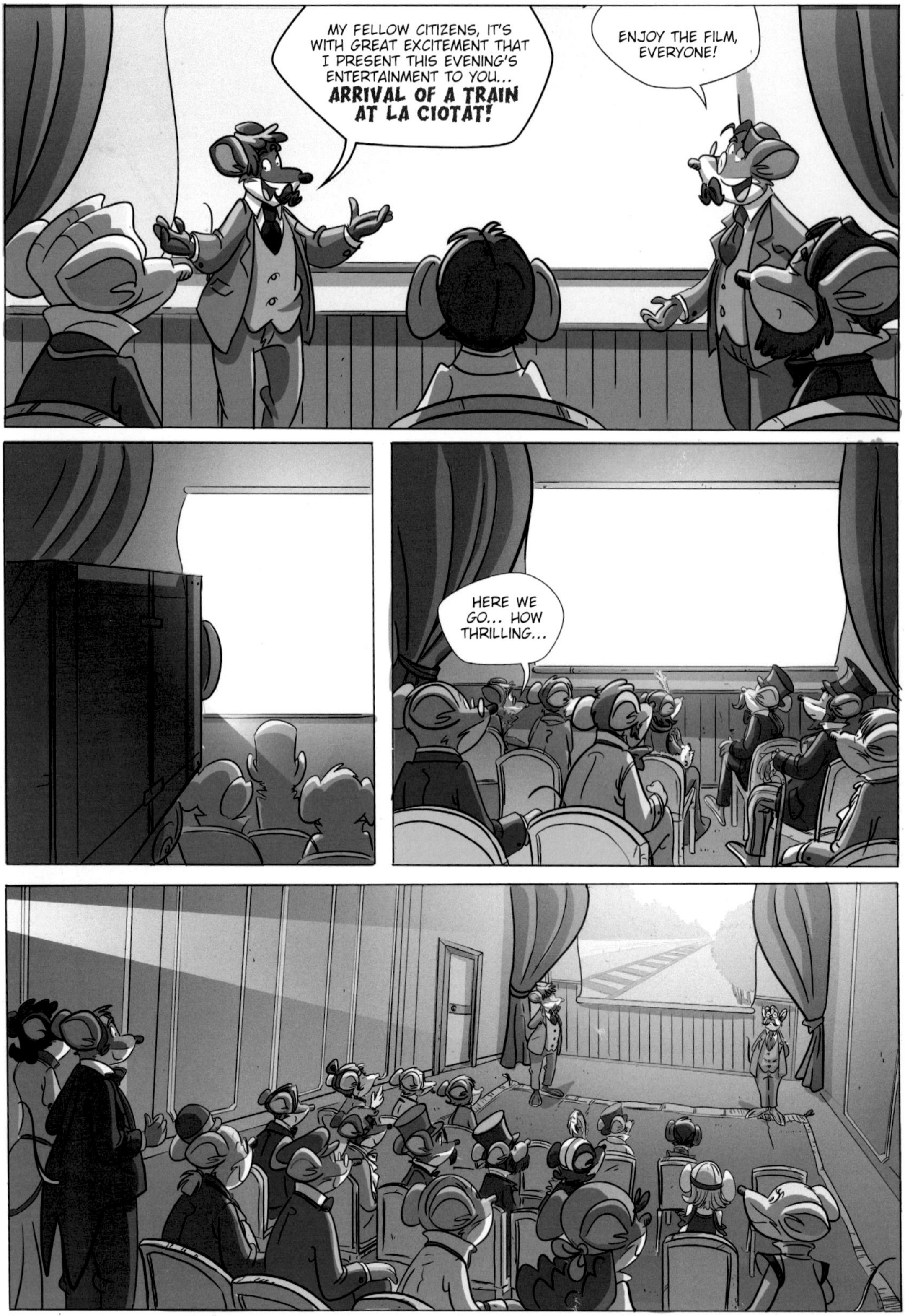

MY FELLOW CITIZENS, IT'S WITH GREAT EXCITEMENT THAT I PRESENT THIS EVENING'S ENTERTAINMENT TO YOU... ARRIVAL OF A TRAIN AT LA CIOTAT!
ENJOY THE FILM, EVERYONE!
HERE WE GO... HOW THRILLING...

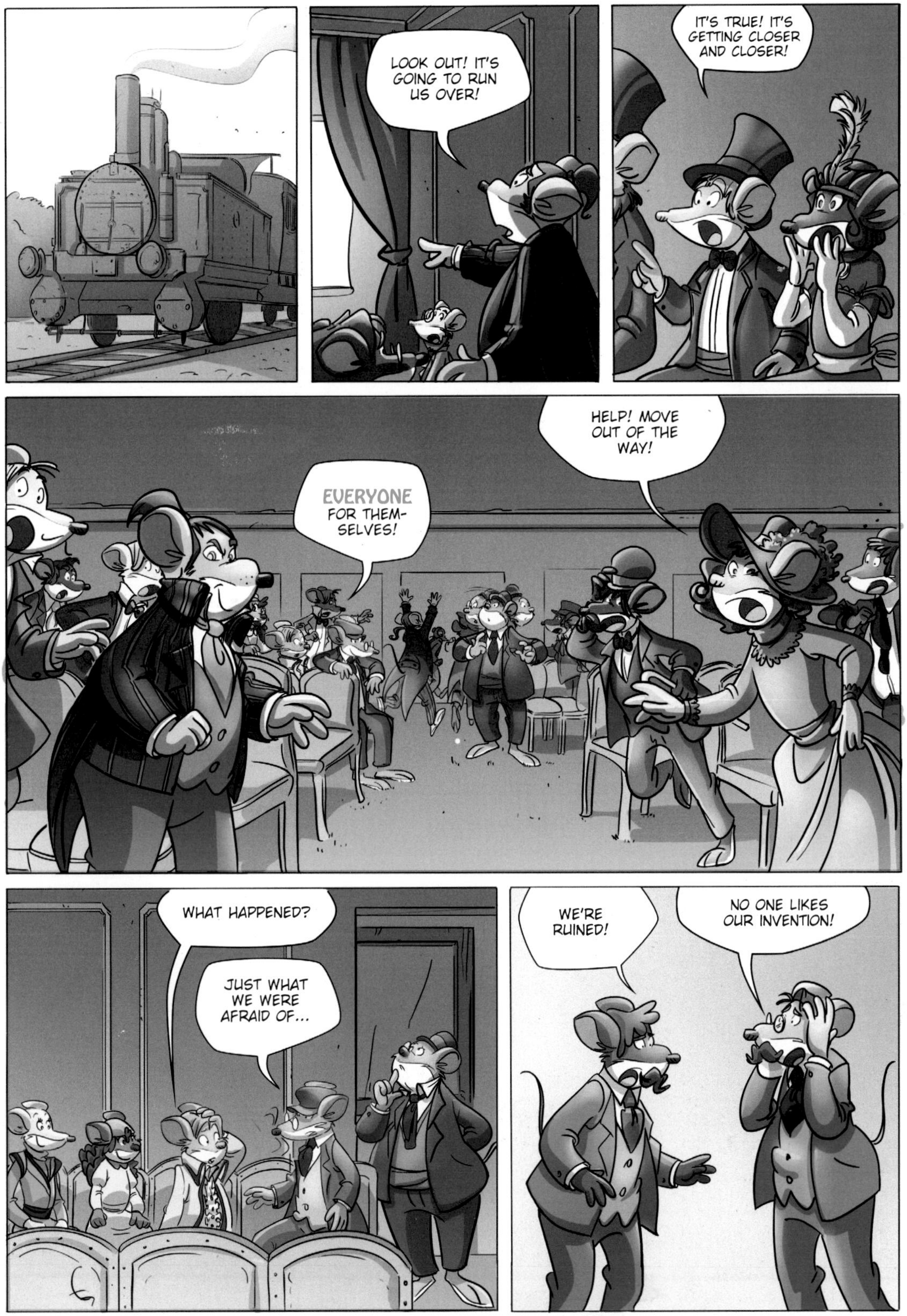
LOOK OUT! IT'S GOING TO RUN US OVER!
IT'S TRUE! IT'S GETTING CLOSER AND CLOSER!
EVERYONE FOR THEMSELVES!
HELP! MOVE OUT OF THE WAY!
WHAT HAPPENED?
JUST WHAT WE WERE AFRAID OF...
WE'RE RUINED!
NO ONE LIKES OUR INVENTION!

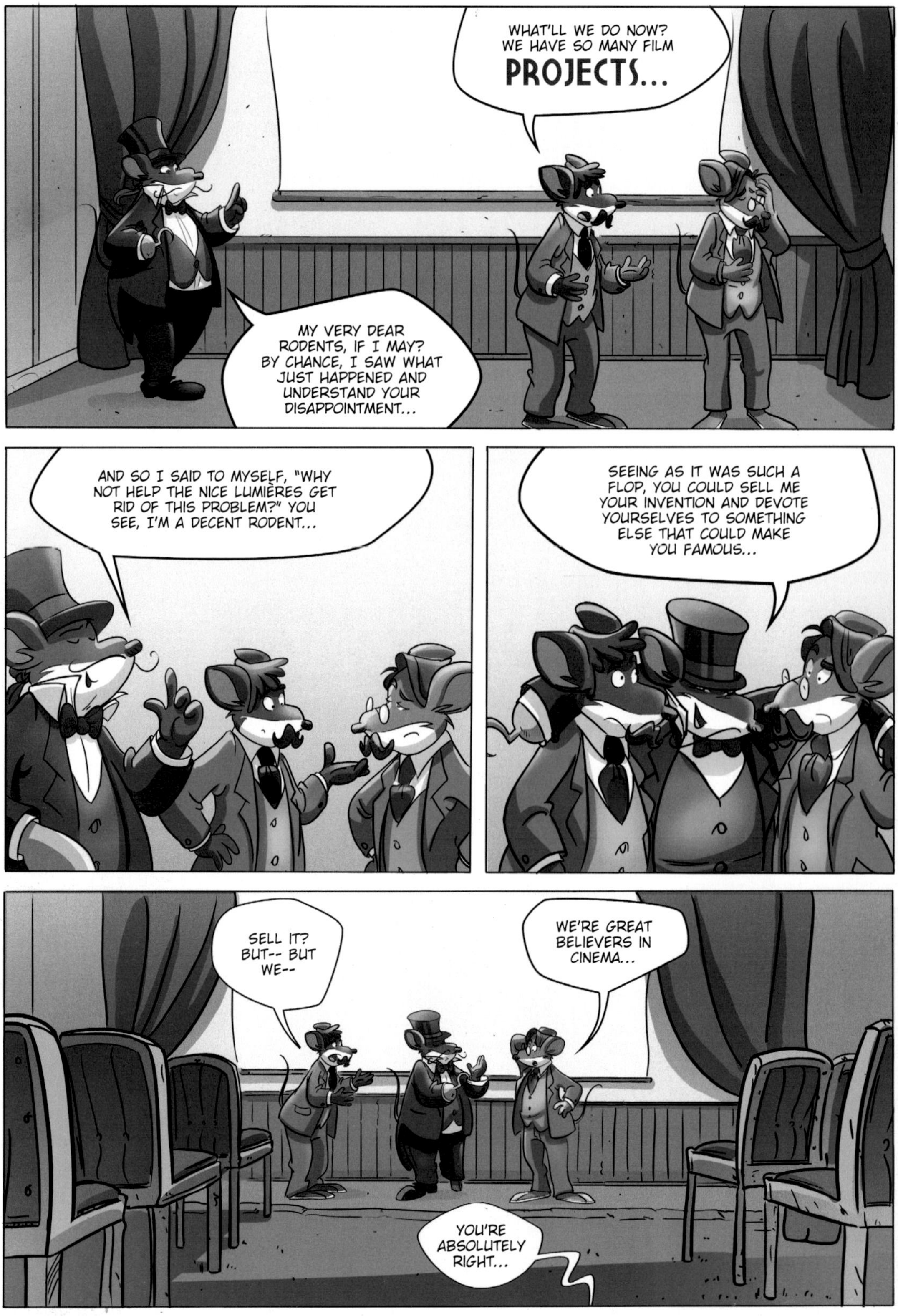
WHAT'LL WE DO NOW? WE HAVE SO MANY FILM PROJECTS...
MY VERY DEAR RODENTS, IF I MAY? BY CHANCE, I SAW WHAT JUST HAPPENED AND UNDERSTAND YOUR DISAPPOINTMENT...
AND SO I SAID TO MYSELF, "WHY NOT HELP THE NICE LUMIÈRES GET RID OF THIS PROBLEM?" YOU SEE, I'M A DECENT RODENT...
SEEING AS IT WAS SUCH A FLOP, YOU COULD SELL ME YOUR INVENTION AND DEVOTE YOURSELVES TO SOMETHING ELSE THAT COULD MAKE YOU FAMOUS...
SELL IT? BUT-- BUT WE--
WE'RE GREAT BELIEVERS IN CINEMA...
YOU'RE ABSOLUTELY RIGHT...

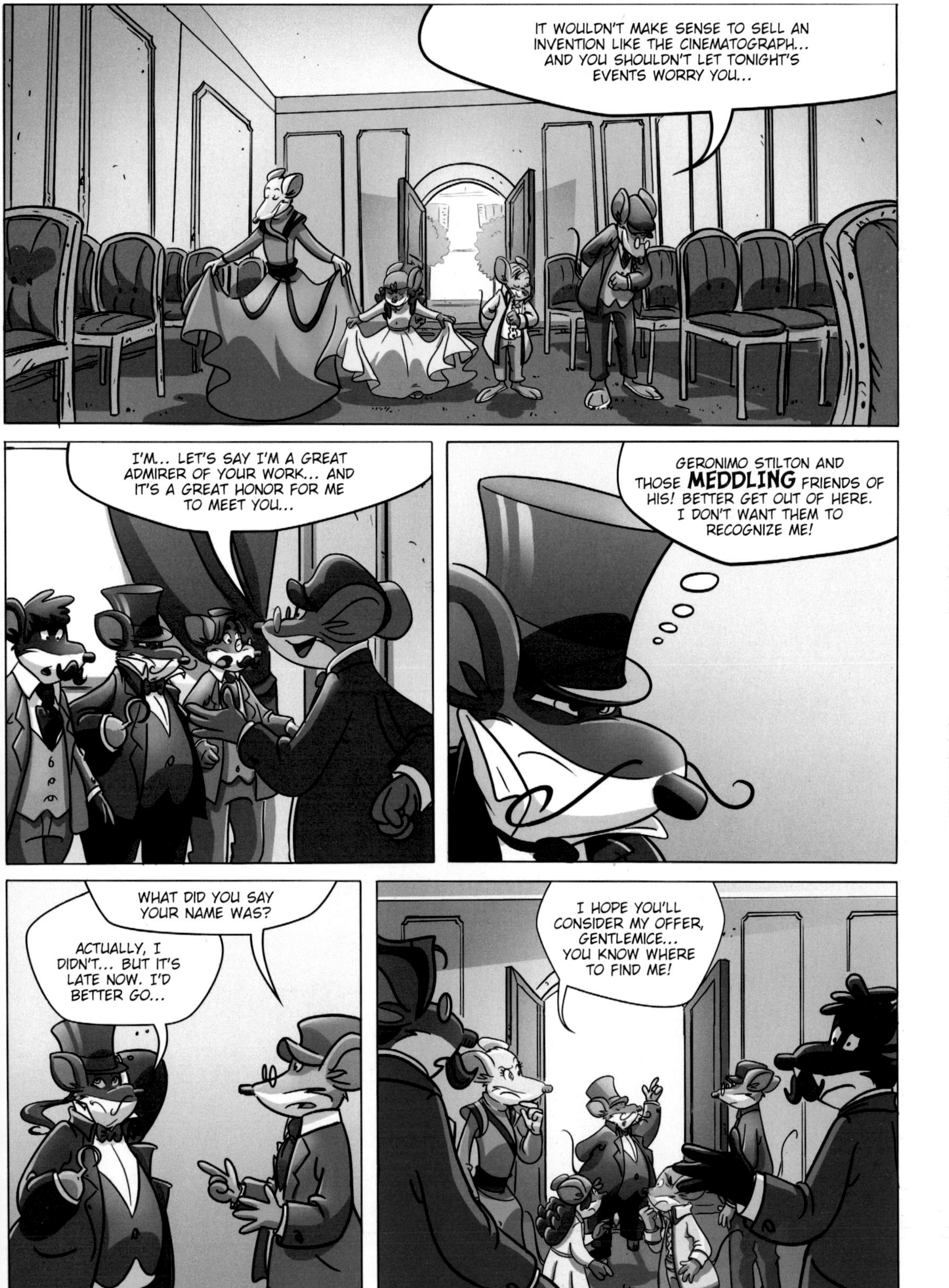
IT WOULDN'T MAKE SENSE TO SELL AN INVENTION LIKE THE CINEMATOGRAPH... AND YOU SHOULDN'T LET TONIGHT'S EVENTS WORRY YOU...
I'M... LET'S SAY I'M A GREAT ADMIRER OF YOUR WORK... AND IT'S A GREAT HONOR FOR ME TO MEET YOU...
GERONIMO STILTON AND THOSE MEDDLING FRIENDS OF HIS! BETTER GET OUT OF HERE. I DON'T WANT THEM TO RECOGNIZE ME!
WHAT DID YOU SAY YOUR NAME WAS?
ACTUALLY, I DIDN'T... BUT IT'S LATE NOW. I'D BETTER GO...
I HOPE YOU'LL CONSIDER MY OFFER, GENTLEMICE... YOU KNOW WHERE TO FIND ME!

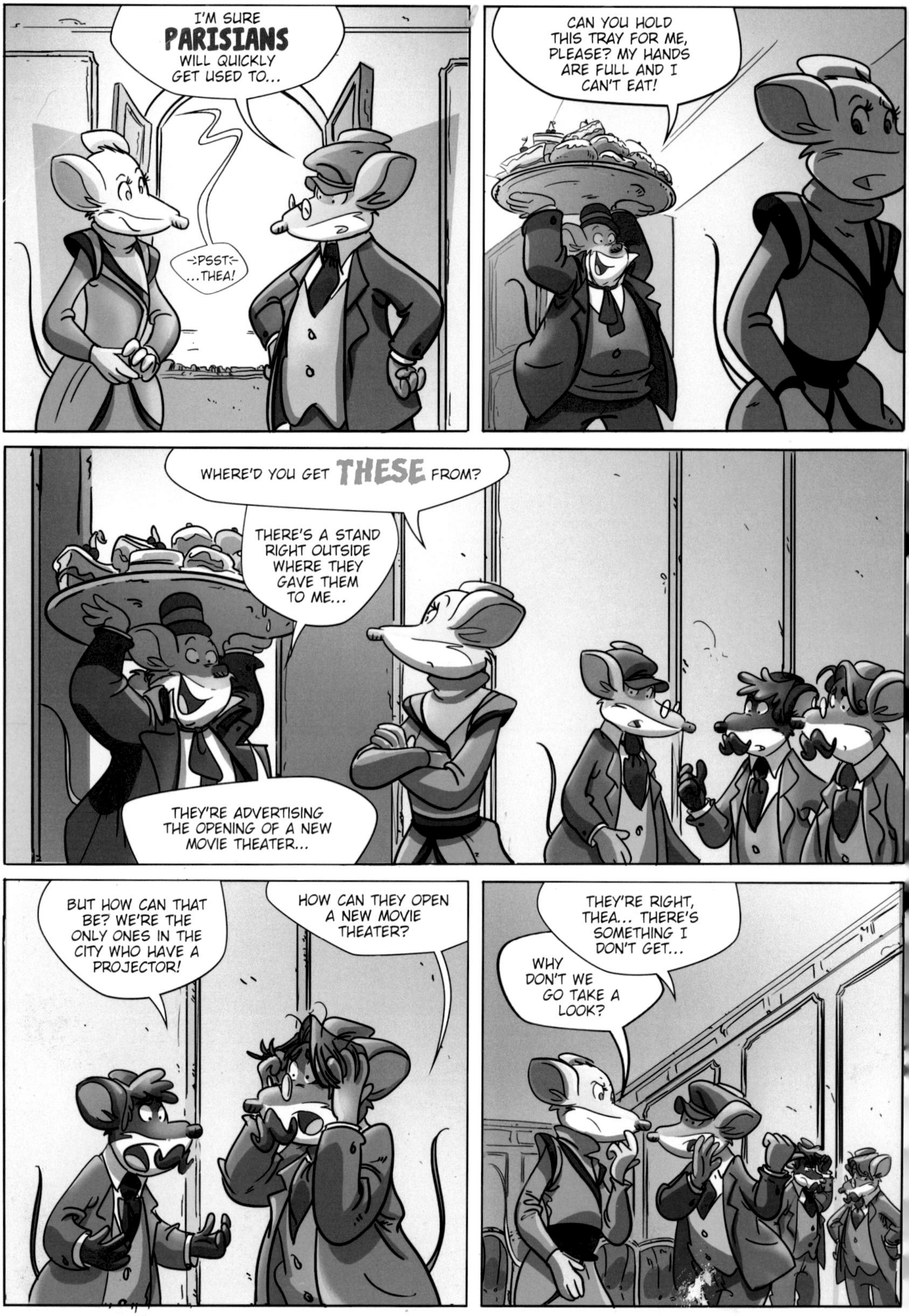
I'M SURE PARISIANS WILL QUICKLY GET USED TO...
-PSST!- ...THEA!
CAN YOU HOLD THIS TRAY FOR ME, PLEASE? MY HANDS ARE FULL AND I CAN'T EAT!
WHERE'D YOU GET THESE FROM?
THERE'S A STAND RIGHT OUTSIDE WHERE THEY GAVE THEM TO ME...
THEY'RE ADVERTISING THE OPENING OF A NEW MOVIE THEATER...
BUT HOW CAN THAT BE? WE'RE THE ONLY ONES IN THE CITY WHO HAVE A PROJECTOR!
HOW CAN THEY OPEN A NEW MOVIE THEATER?
THEY'RE RIGHT, THEA... THERE'S SOMETHING I DON'T GET...
WHY DON'T WE GO TAKE A LOOK?

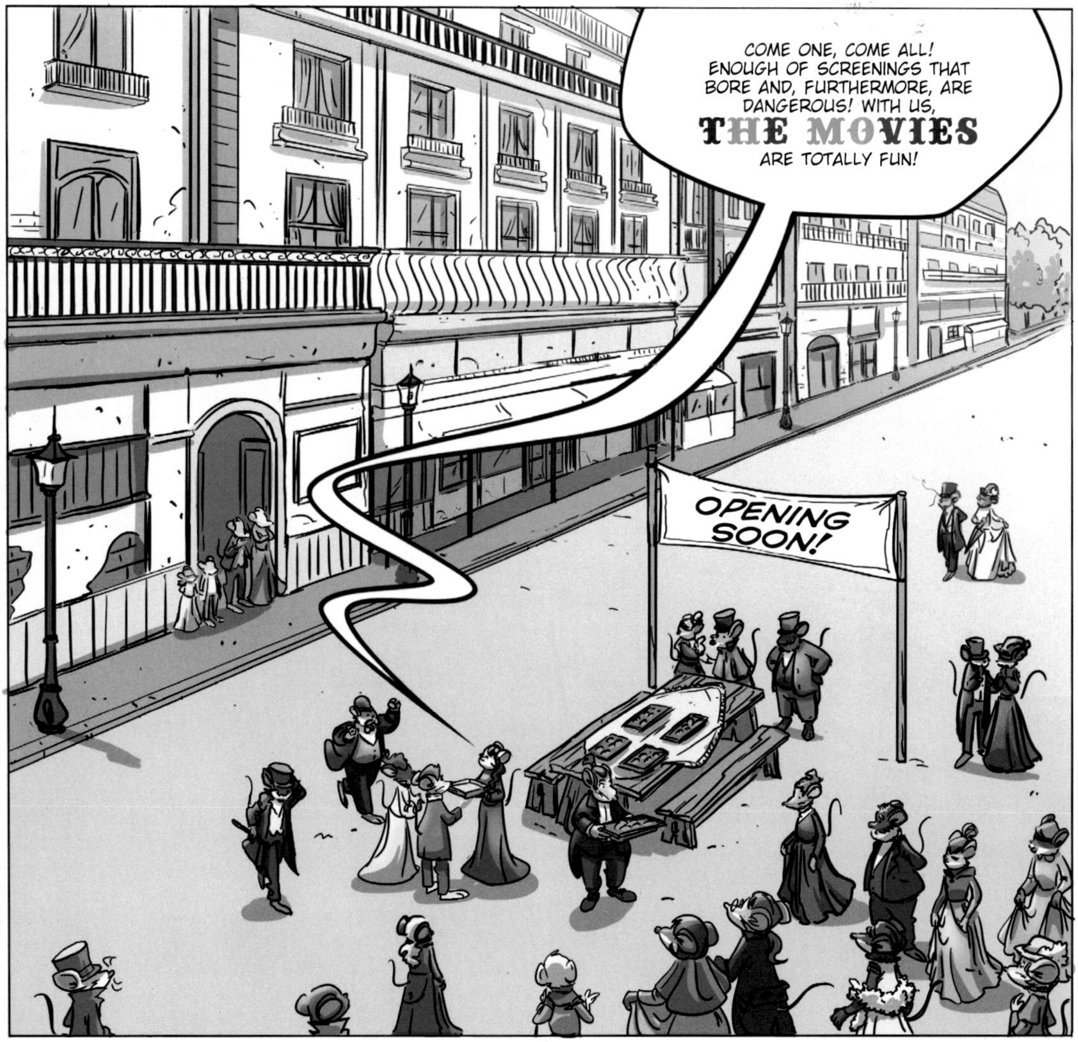
COME ONE, COME ALL! ENOUGH OF SCREENINGS THAT BORE AND, FURTHERMORE, ARE DANGEROUS! WITH US, THE MOVIES ARE TOTALLY FUN!
OPENING SOON!

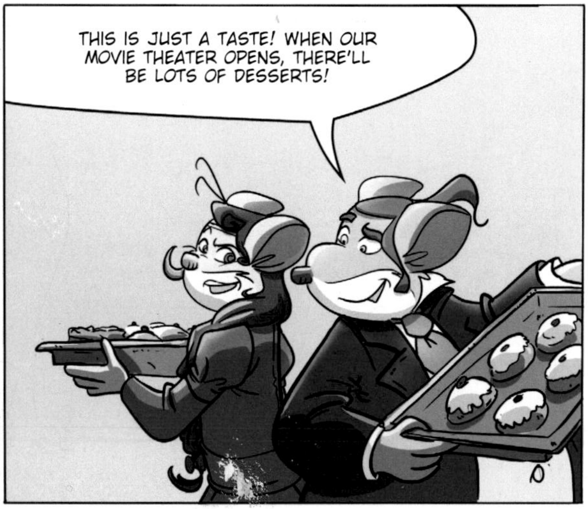
THIS IS JUST A TASTE! WHEN OUR MOVIE THEATER OPENS, THERE'LL BE LOTS OF DESSERTS!

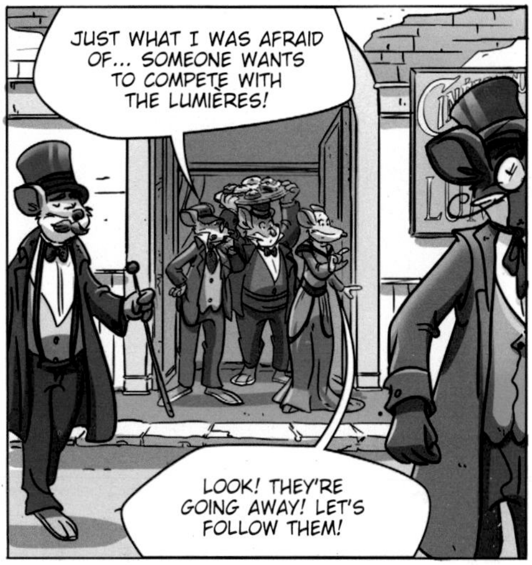
JUST WHAT I WAS AFRAID OF... SOMEONE WANTS TO COMPETE WITH THE LUMIÈRES!
LOOK! THEY'RE GOING AWAY! LET'S FOLLOW THEM!

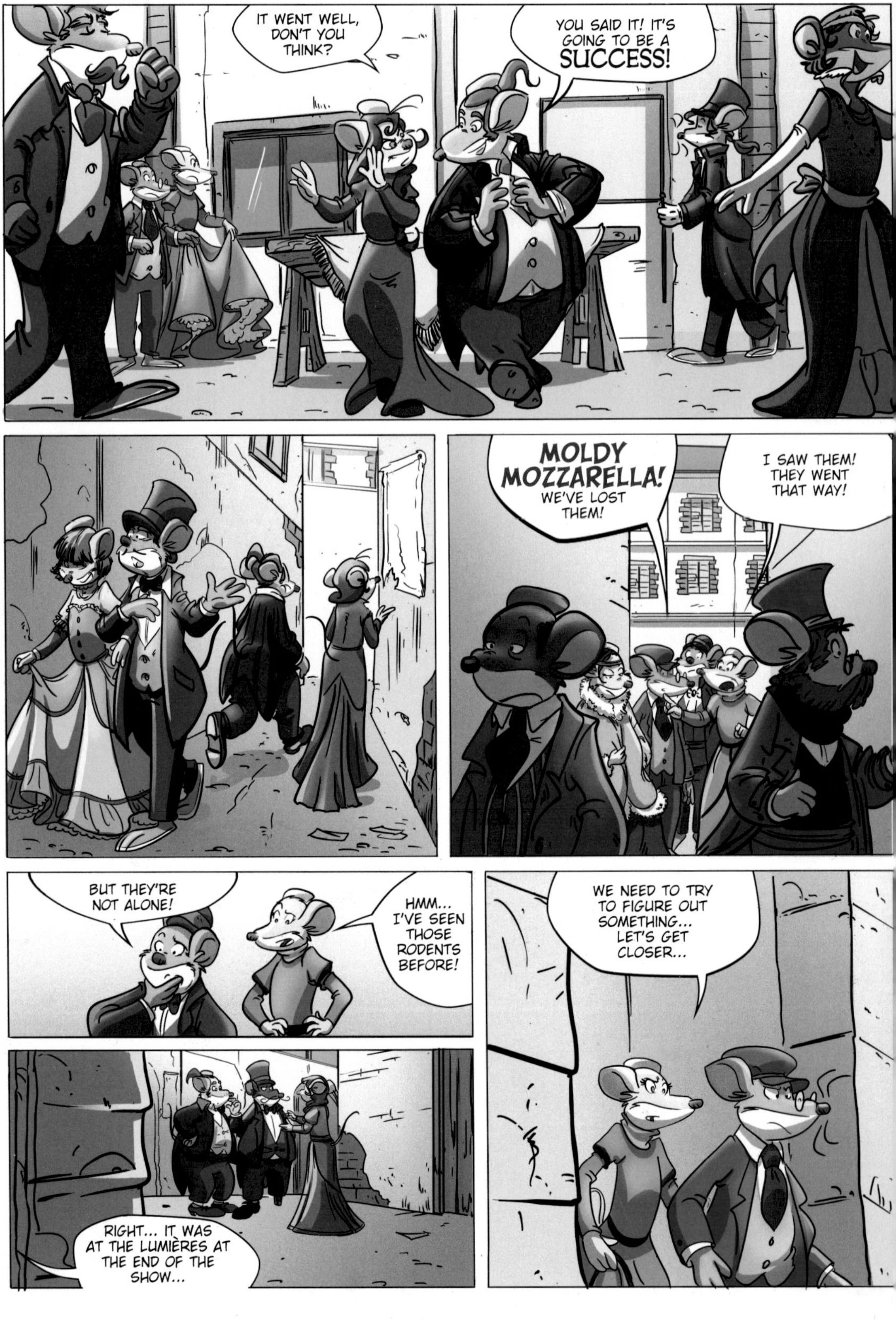

IT WENT WELL, DON'T YOU THINK?
YOU SAID IT! IT'S GOING TO BE A SUCCESS!
MOLDY MOZZARELLA! WE'VE LOST THEM!
I SAW THEM! THEY WENT THAT WAY!
BUT THEY'RE NOT ALONE!
HMM... I'VE SEEN THOSE RODENTS BEFORE!
RIGHT... IT WAS AT THE LUMIÈRES AT THE END OF THE SHOW...
WE NEED TO TRY TO FIGURE OUT SOMETHING... LET'S GET CLOSER...

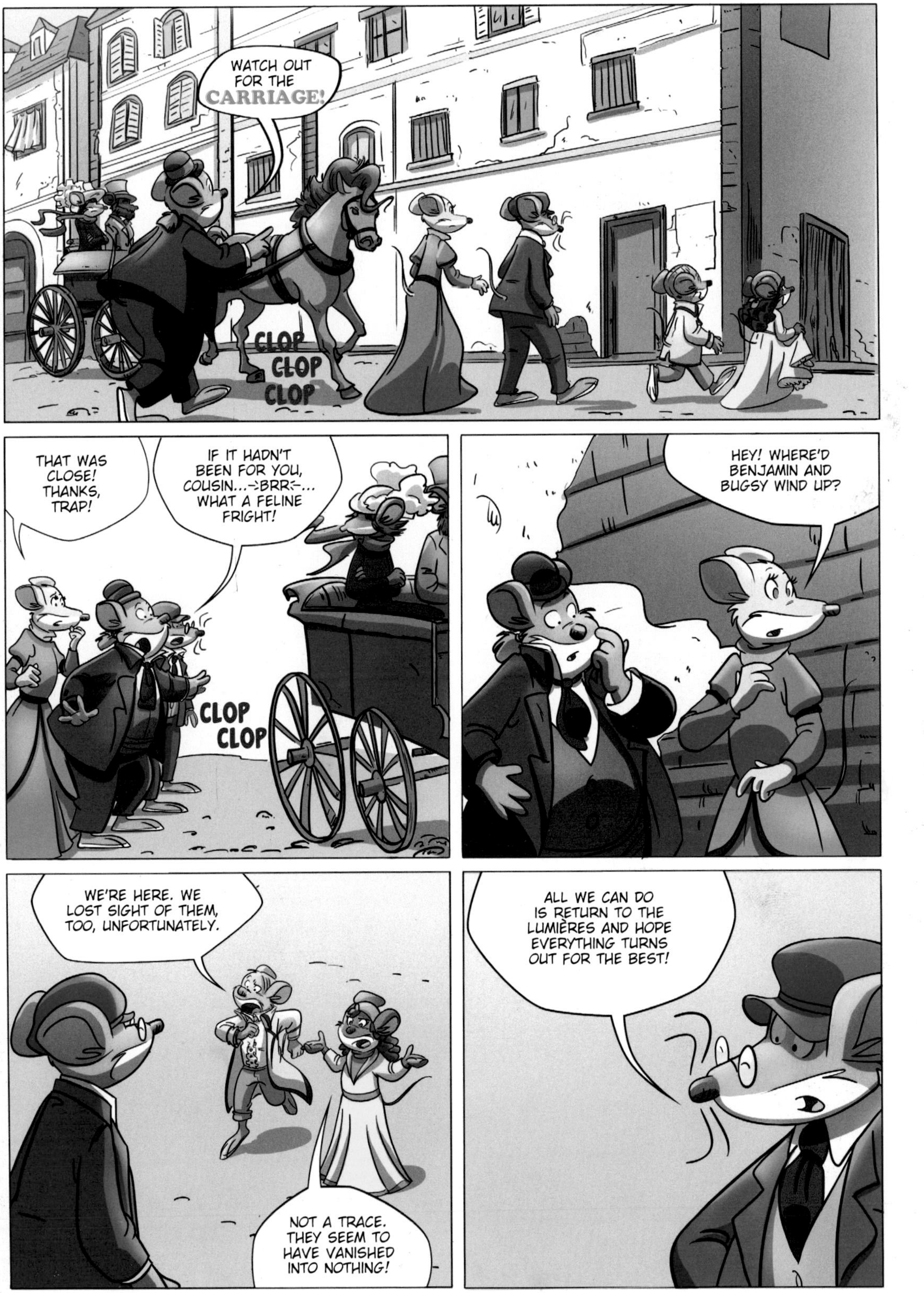
WATCH OUT FOR THE CARRIAGE!
CLOP CLOP CLOP
THAT WAS CLOSE! THANKS, TRAP!
IF IT HADN'T BEEN FOR YOU, COUSIN... →BRR←... WHAT A FELINE FRIGHT!
CLOP CLOP
HEY! WHERE'D BENJAMIN AND BUGSY WIND UP?
WE'RE HERE. WE LOST SIGHT OF THEM, TOO, UNFORTUNATELY.
NOT A TRACE. THEY SEEM TO HAVE VANISHED INTO NOTHING!
ALL WE CAN DO IS RETURN TO THE LUMIÈRES AND HOPE EVERYTHING TURNS OUT FOR THE BEST!

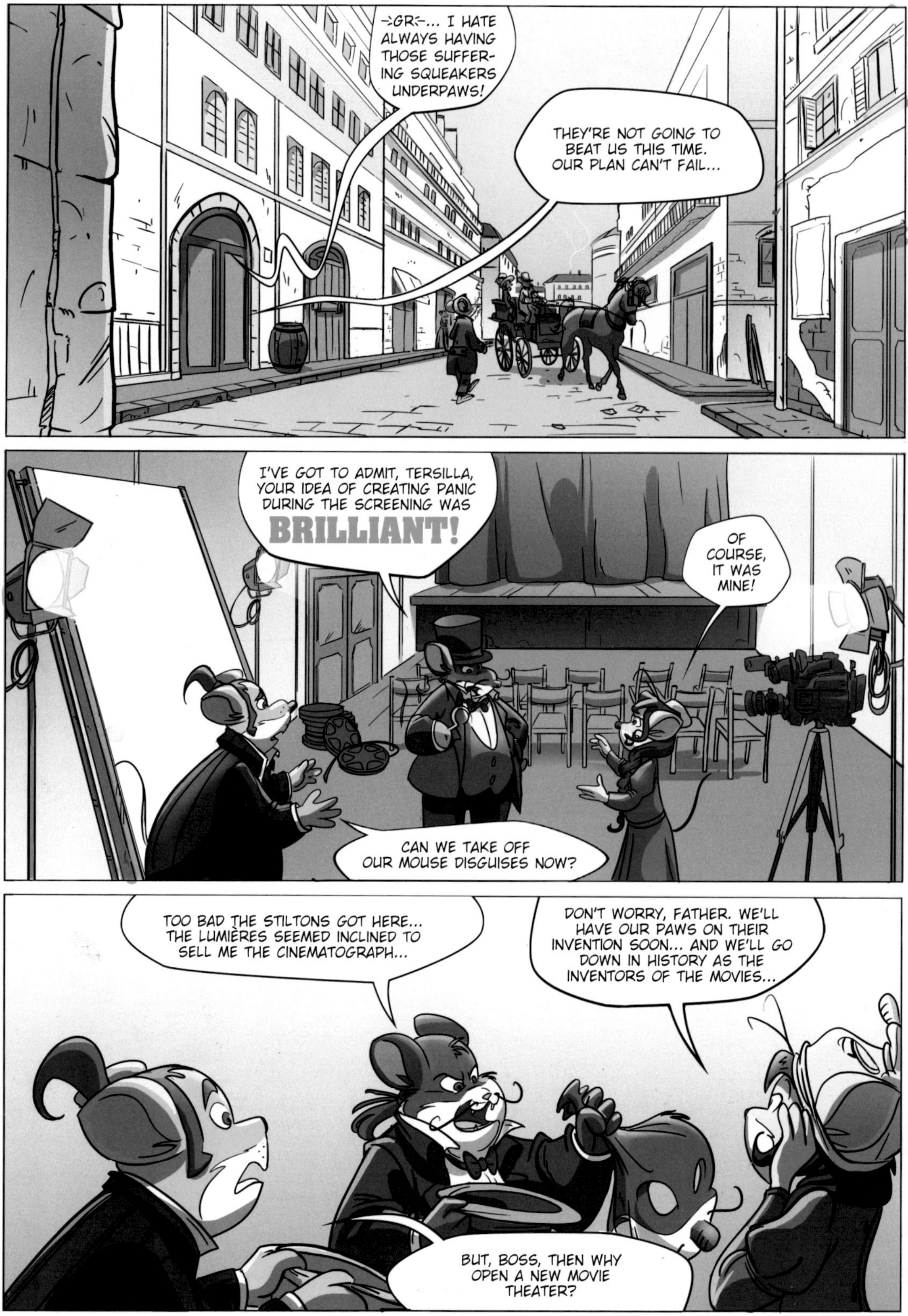
GR... I HATE ALWAYS HAVING THOSE SUFFERING SQUEAKERS UNDERPAWS!
THEY'RE NOT GOING TO BEAT US THIS TIME. OUR PLAN CAN'T FAIL...
I'VE GOT TO ADMIT, TERSILLA, YOUR IDEA OF CREATING PANIC DURING THE SCREENING WAS BRILLIANT!
OF COURSE, IT WAS MINE!
CAN WE TAKE OFF OUR MOUSE DISGUISES NOW?
TOO BAD THE STILTONS GOT HERE... THE LUMIÈRES SEEMED INCLINED TO SELL ME THE CINEMATOGRAPH...
DON'T WORRY, FATHER. WE'LL HAVE OUR PAWS ON THEIR INVENTION SOON... AND WE'LL GO DOWN IN HISTORY AS THE INVENTORS OF THE MOVIES...
BUT, BOSS, THEN WHY OPEN A NEW MOVIE THEATER?

BONZO, I ALWAYS HAVE TO EXPLAIN EVERYTHING TO YOU! WE'RE GOING TO BUILD A MOVIE HOUSE IN THIS OLD THEATER THAT'S COMPLETELY DIFFERENT FROM THE LUMIÈRES...

DIFFERENT?

SWEETS, CANDIES, PARTY ATMOSPHERE, AND FUNNY FILMS... IT'LL BE A PERFORMANCE FOR PARISIANS!

WE'LL SHOW THESE SHORT COMEDY FILMS THAT HAVEN'T YET BEEN SEEN AT THIS TIME...

AND THEN, ONCE WE'VE DRAWN THEM HERE...

WE'LL SHOW THEM A MOVIE ABOUT THE LIFE OF THE RULER OF **THE PIRATE CATS...**

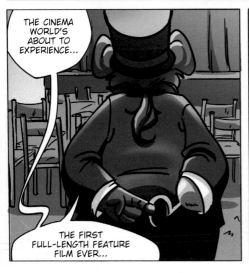

THE CINEMA WORLD'S ABOUT TO EXPERIENCE...

THE FIRST FULL-LENGTH FEATURE FILM EVER...

"THE GREAT CATARDONE!"

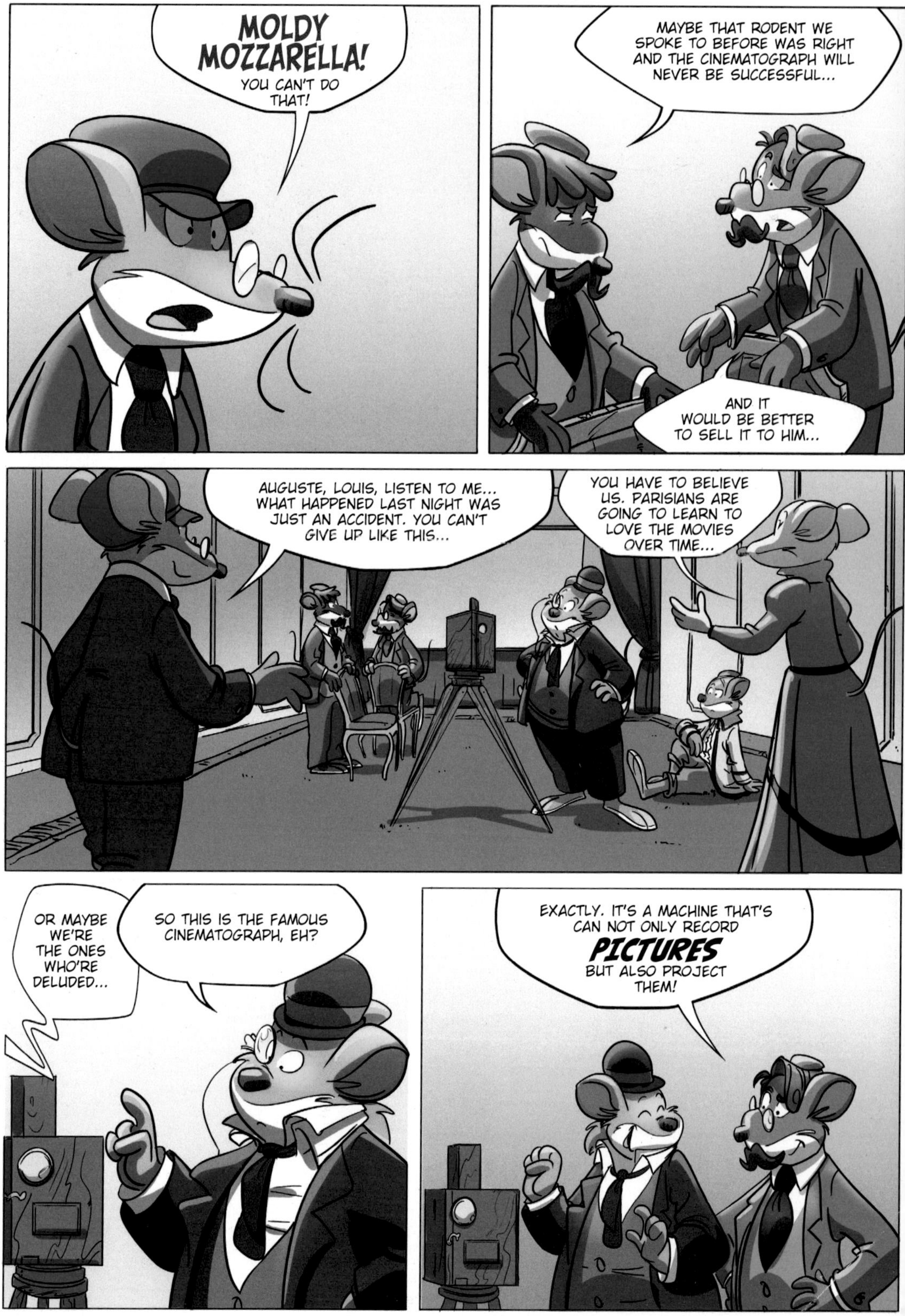
MOLDY MOZZARELLA! YOU CAN'T DO THAT!
MAYBE THAT RODENT WE SPOKE TO BEFORE WAS RIGHT AND THE CINEMATOGRAPH WILL NEVER BE SUCCESSFUL...
AND IT WOULD BE BETTER TO SELL IT TO HIM...
AUGUSTE, LOUIS, LISTEN TO ME... WHAT HAPPENED LAST NIGHT WAS JUST AN ACCIDENT. YOU CAN'T GIVE UP LIKE THIS...
YOU HAVE TO BELIEVE US. PARISIANS ARE GOING TO LEARN TO LOVE THE MOVIES OVER TIME...
OR MAYBE WE'RE THE ONES WHO'RE DELUDED...
SO THIS IS THE FAMOUS CINEMATOGRAPH, EH?
EXACTLY. IT'S A MACHINE THAT'S CAN NOT ONLY RECORD PICTURES BUT ALSO PROJECT THEM!

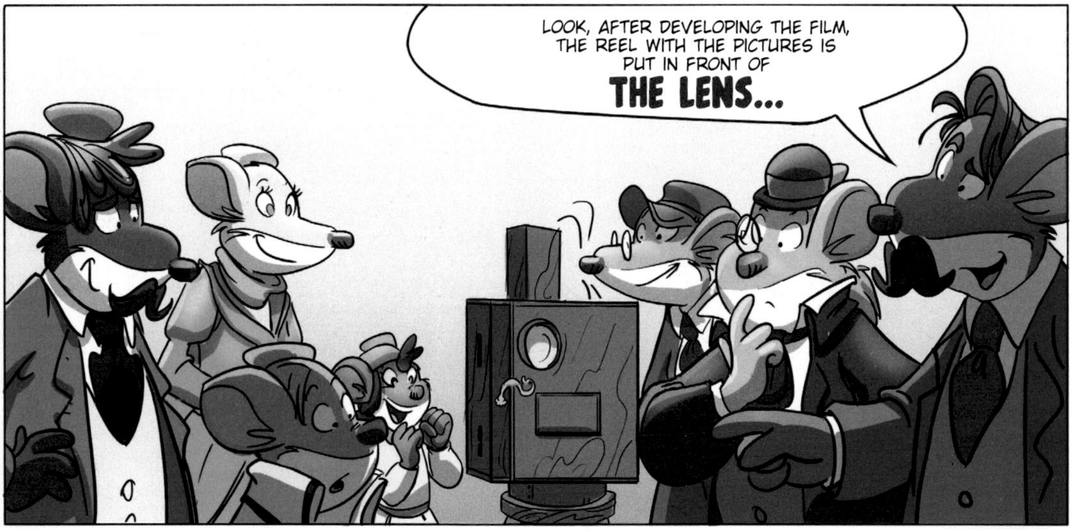
LOOK, AFTER DEVELOPING THE FILM, THE REEL WITH THE PICTURES IS PUT IN FRONT OF
THE LENS...

THE CINEMATOGRAPH REALLY OWES ITS FAME TO THE PROJECTING MECHANISM. ONCE THE FILM IS PLACED INSIDE, A DEVICE MAKES THE IMAGES FLOW ONE AFTER THE OTHER WITHOUT SHOWING THEM AS THEY PASS FROM ONE TO THE NEXT, THUS CREATING THE SENSATION OF MOVEMENT.

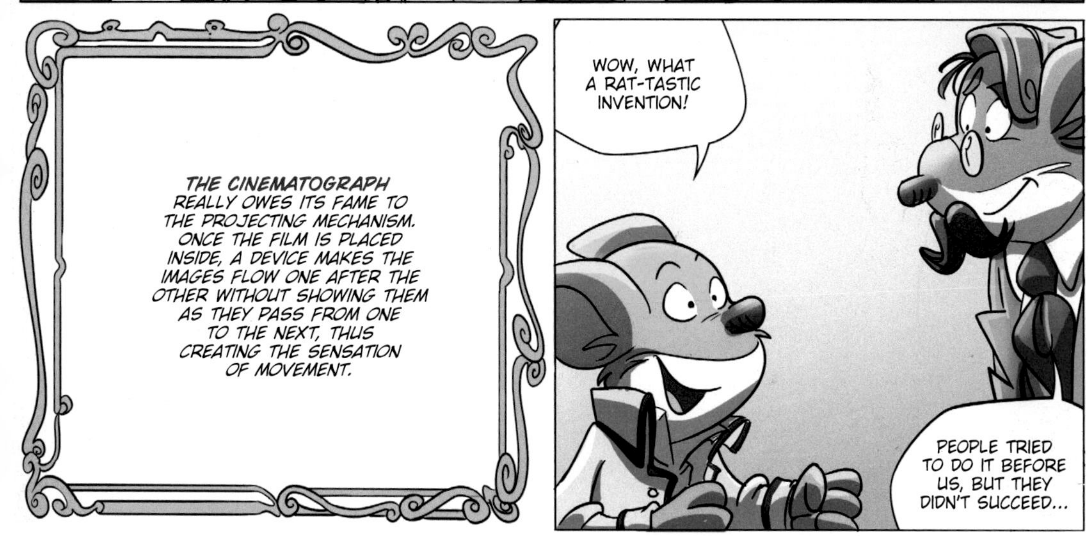
WOW, WHAT A RAT-TASTIC INVENTION!
PEOPLE TRIED TO DO IT BEFORE US, BUT THEY DIDN'T SUCCEED...

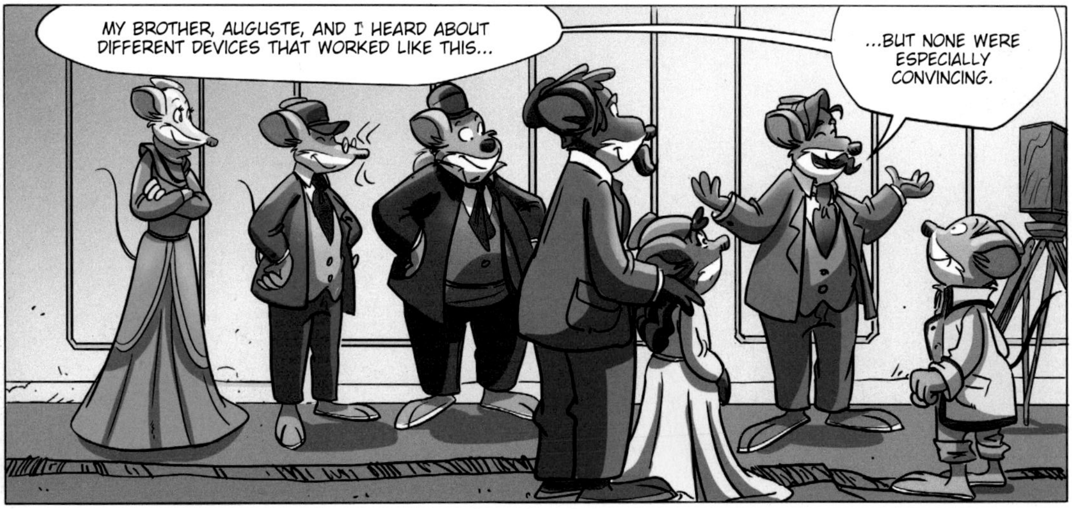
MY BROTHER, AUGUSTE, AND I HEARD ABOUT DIFFERENT DEVICES THAT WORKED LIKE THIS...
...BUT NONE WERE ESPECIALLY CONVINCING.

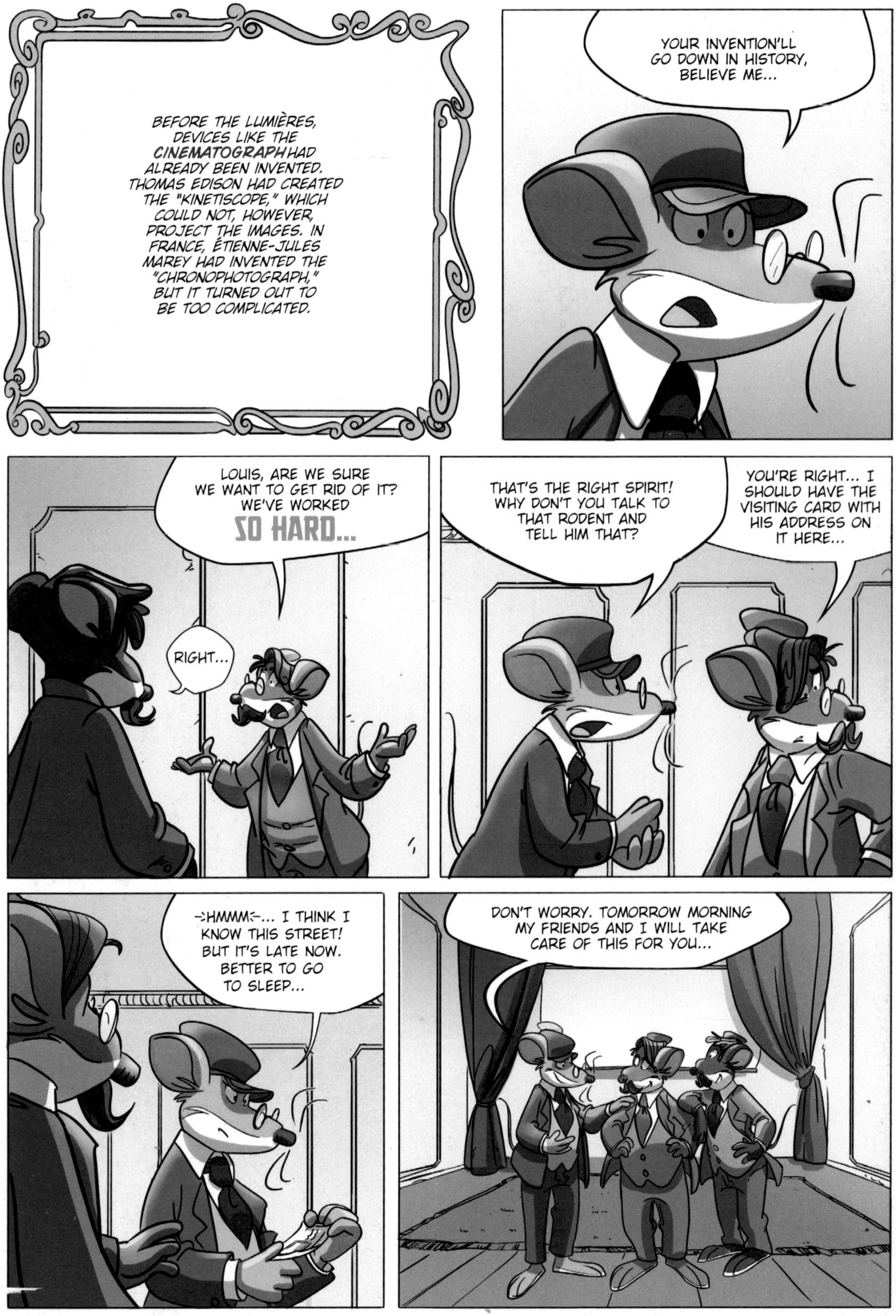
BEFORE THE LUMIÈRES, DEVICES LIKE THE CINEMATOGRAPH HAD ALREADY BEEN INVENTED. THOMAS EDISON HAD CREATED THE "KINETISCOPE," WHICH COULD NOT, HOWEVER, PROJECT THE IMAGES. IN FRANCE, ÉTIENNE-JULES MAREY HAD INVENTED THE "CHRONOPHOTOGRAPH," BUT IT TURNED OUT TO BE TOO COMPLICATED.
YOUR INVENTION'LL GO DOWN IN HISTORY, BELIEVE ME...
LOUIS, ARE WE SURE WE WANT TO GET RID OF IT? WE'VE WORKED SO HARD...
RIGHT...
THAT'S THE RIGHT SPIRIT! WHY DON'T YOU TALK TO THAT RODENT AND TELL HIM THAT?
YOU'RE RIGHT... I SHOULD HAVE THE VISITING CARD WITH HIS ADDRESS ON IT HERE...
HMMM... I THINK I KNOW THIS STREET! BUT IT'S LATE NOW. BETTER TO GO TO SLEEP...
DON'T WORRY. TOMORROW MORNING MY FRIENDS AND I WILL TAKE CARE OF THIS FOR YOU...

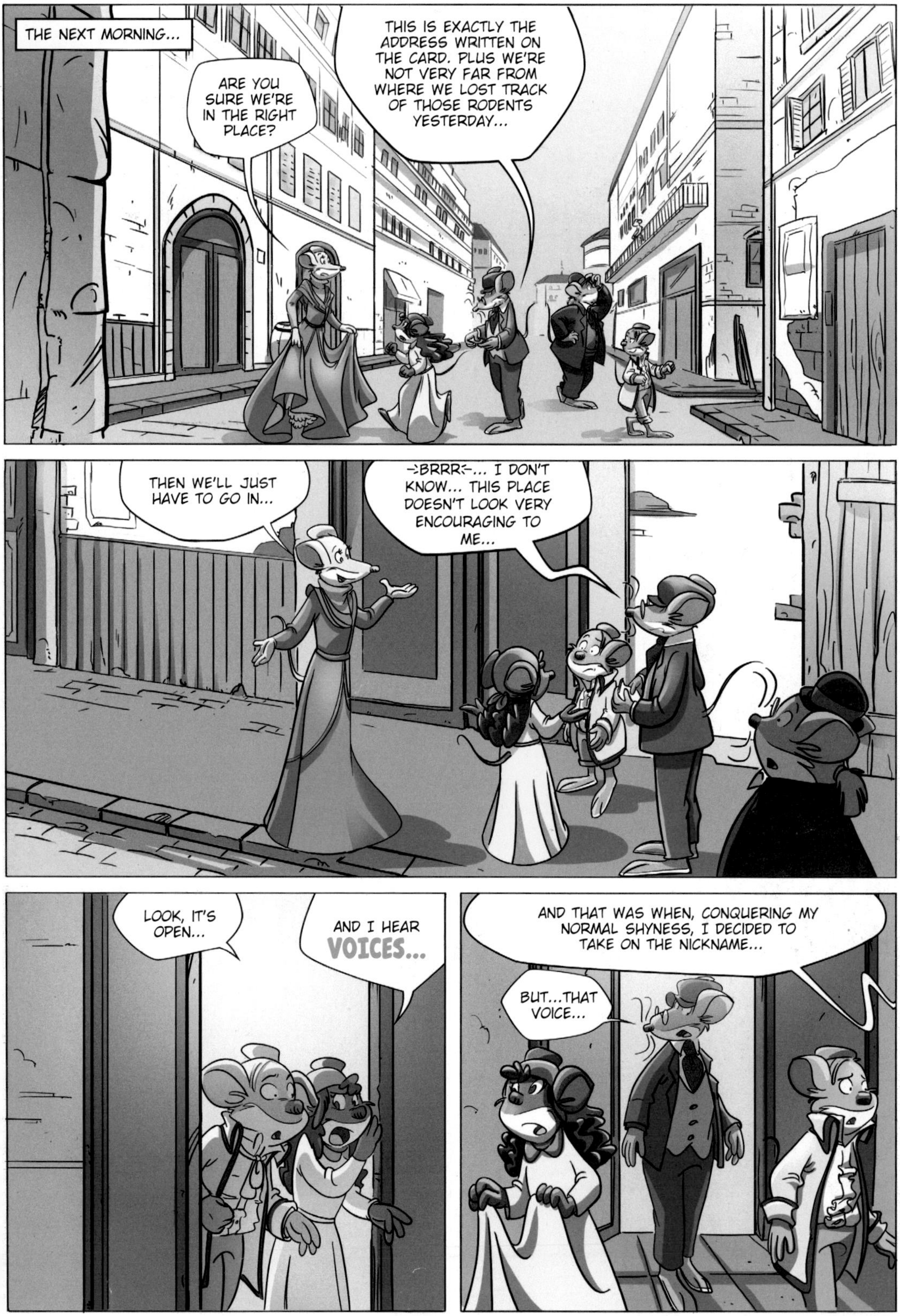
THE NEXT MORNING...
ARE YOU SURE WE'RE IN THE RIGHT PLACE?
THIS IS EXACTLY THE ADDRESS WRITTEN ON THE CARD. PLUS WE'RE NOT VERY FAR FROM WHERE WE LOST TRACK OF THOSE RODENTS YESTERDAY...
THEN WE'LL JUST HAVE TO GO IN...
-BRRR-... I DON'T KNOW... THIS PLACE DOESN'T LOOK VERY ENCOURAGING TO ME...
LOOK, IT'S OPEN...
AND I HEAR VOICES...
AND THAT WAS WHEN, CONQUERING MY NORMAL SHYNESS, I DECIDED TO TAKE ON THE NICKNAME...
BUT...THAT VOICE...

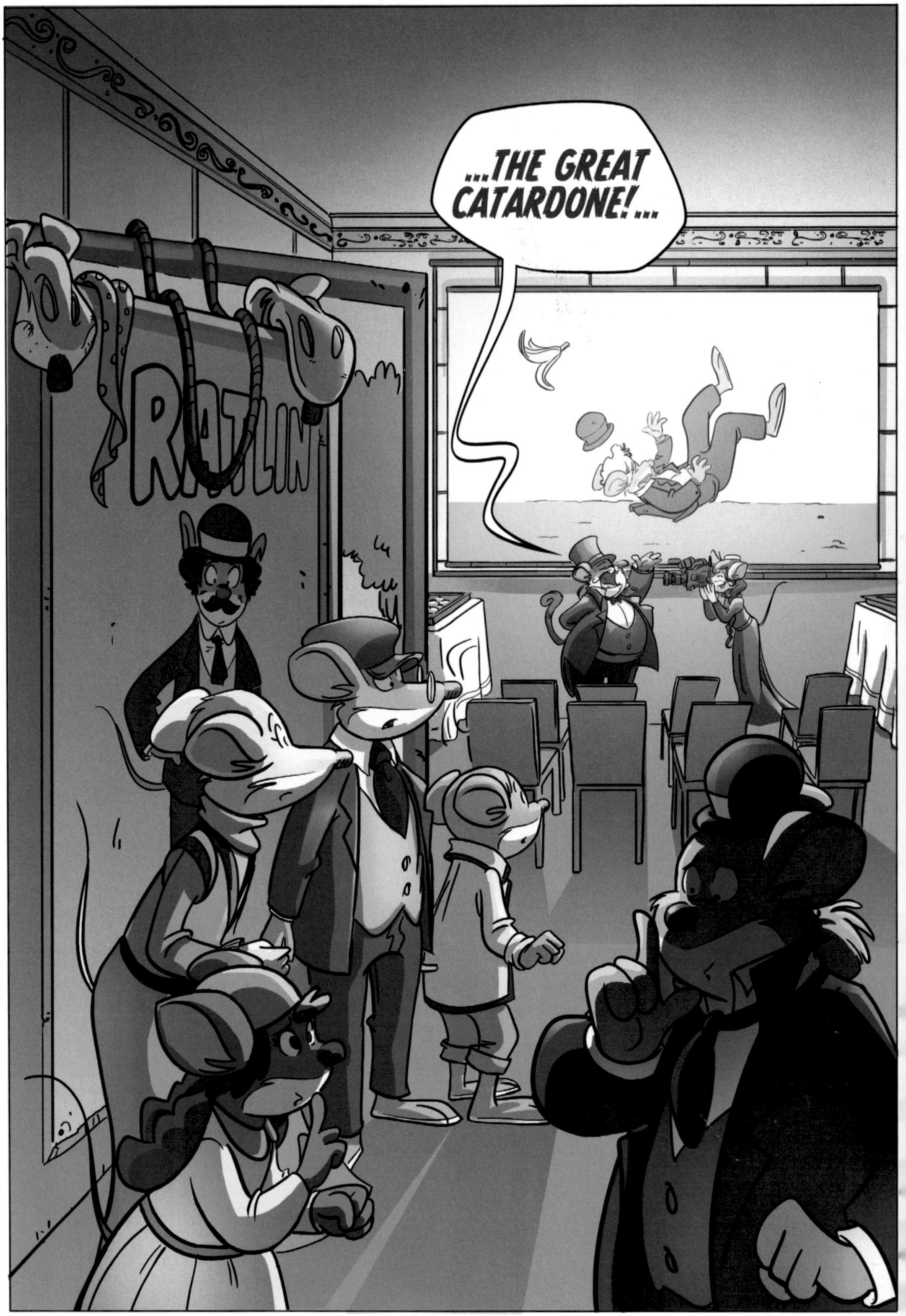
...THE GREAT CATARDONE!...
RATLIN

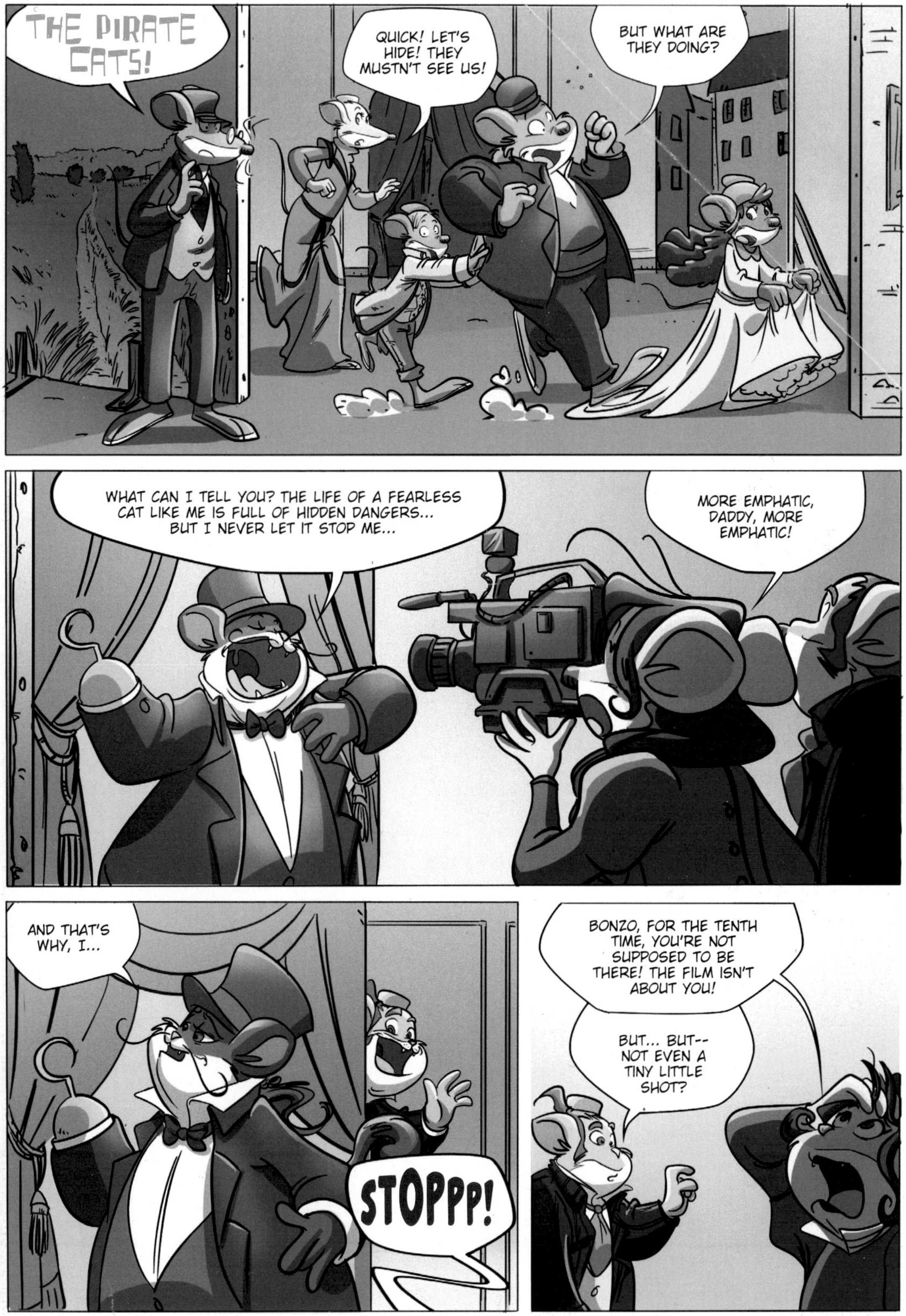
THE PIRATE CATS!
QUICK! LET'S HIDE! THEY MUSTN'T SEE US!
BUT WHAT ARE THEY DOING?
WHAT CAN I TELL YOU? THE LIFE OF A FEARLESS CAT LIKE ME IS FULL OF HIDDEN DANGERS... BUT I NEVER LET IT STOP ME...
MORE EMPHATIC, DADDY, MORE EMPHATIC!
AND THAT'S WHY, I...
STOPPP!
BONZO, FOR THE TENTH TIME, YOU'RE NOT SUPPOSED TO BE THERE! THE FILM ISN'T ABOUT YOU!
BUT... BUT-- NOT EVEN A TINY LITTLE SHOT?

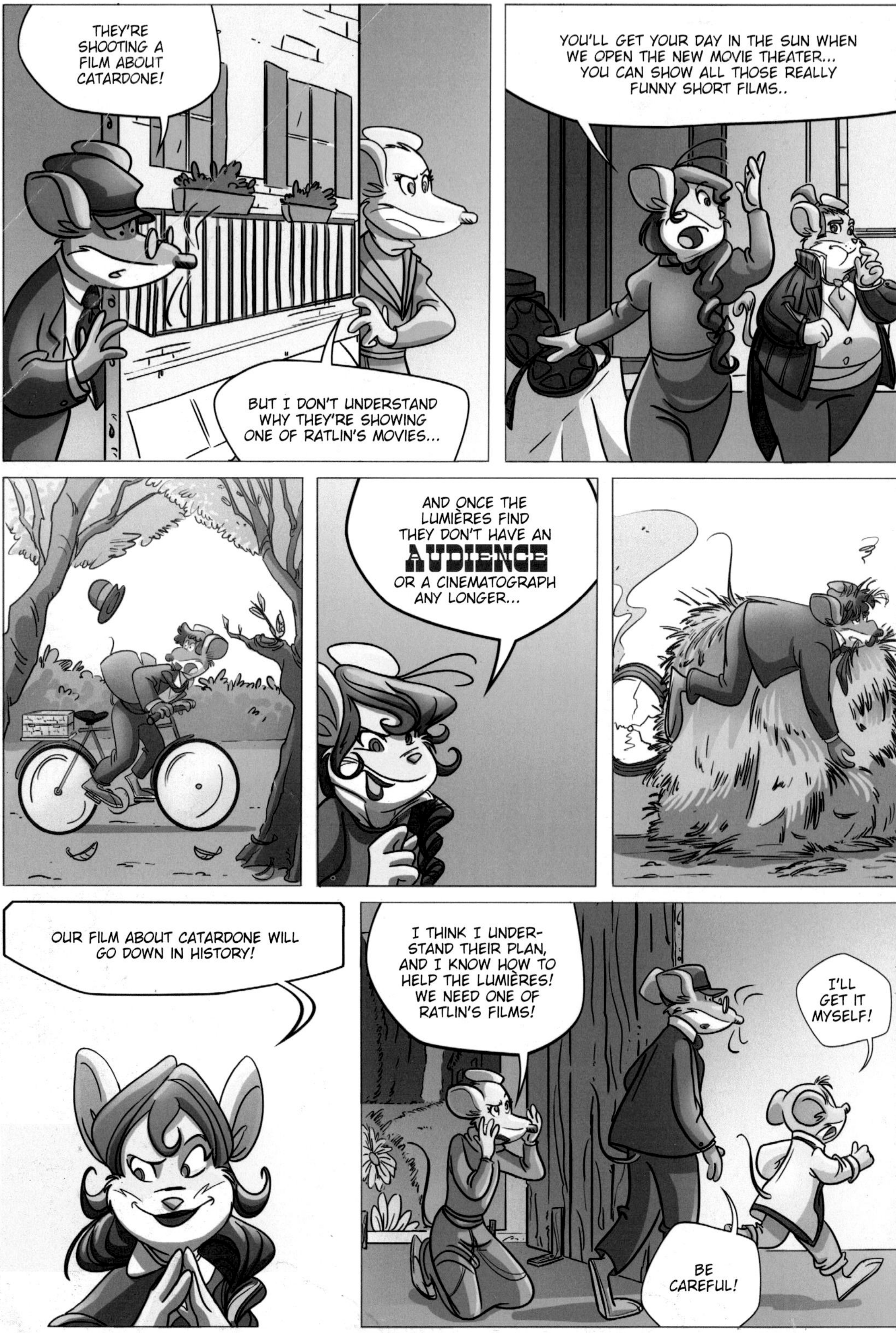
THEY'RE SHOOTING A FILM ABOUT CATARDONE!
BUT I DON'T UNDERSTAND WHY THEY'RE SHOWING ONE OF RATLIN'S MOVIES...
YOU'LL GET YOUR DAY IN THE SUN WHEN WE OPEN THE NEW MOVIE THEATER... YOU CAN SHOW ALL THOSE REALLY FUNNY SHORT FILMS..
AND ONCE THE LUMIÈRES FIND THEY DON'T HAVE AN AUDIENCE OR A CINEMATOGRAPH ANY LONGER...
OUR FILM ABOUT CATARDONE WILL GO DOWN IN HISTORY!
I THINK I UNDER-STAND THEIR PLAN, AND I KNOW HOW TO HELP THE LUMIÈRES! WE NEED ONE OF RATLIN'S FILMS!
I'LL GET IT MYSELF!
BE CAREFUL!

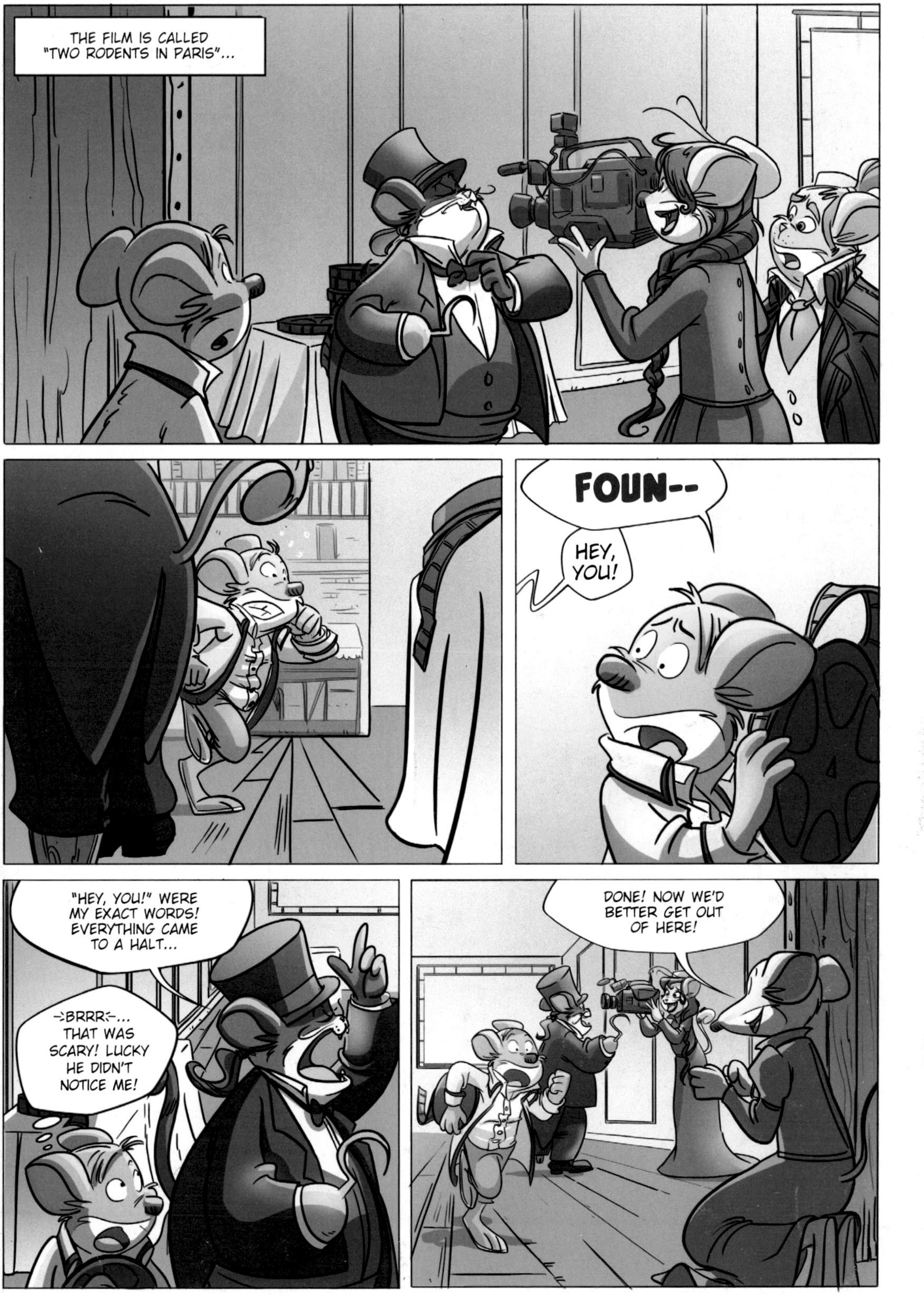
THE FILM IS CALLED "TWO RODENTS IN PARIS"...
FOUN--
HEY, YOU!
"HEY, YOU!" WERE MY EXACT WORDS! EVERYTHING CAME TO A HALT...
-BRRR-... THAT WAS SCARY! LUCKY HE DIDN'T NOTICE ME!
DONE! NOW WE'D BETTER GET OUT OF HERE!

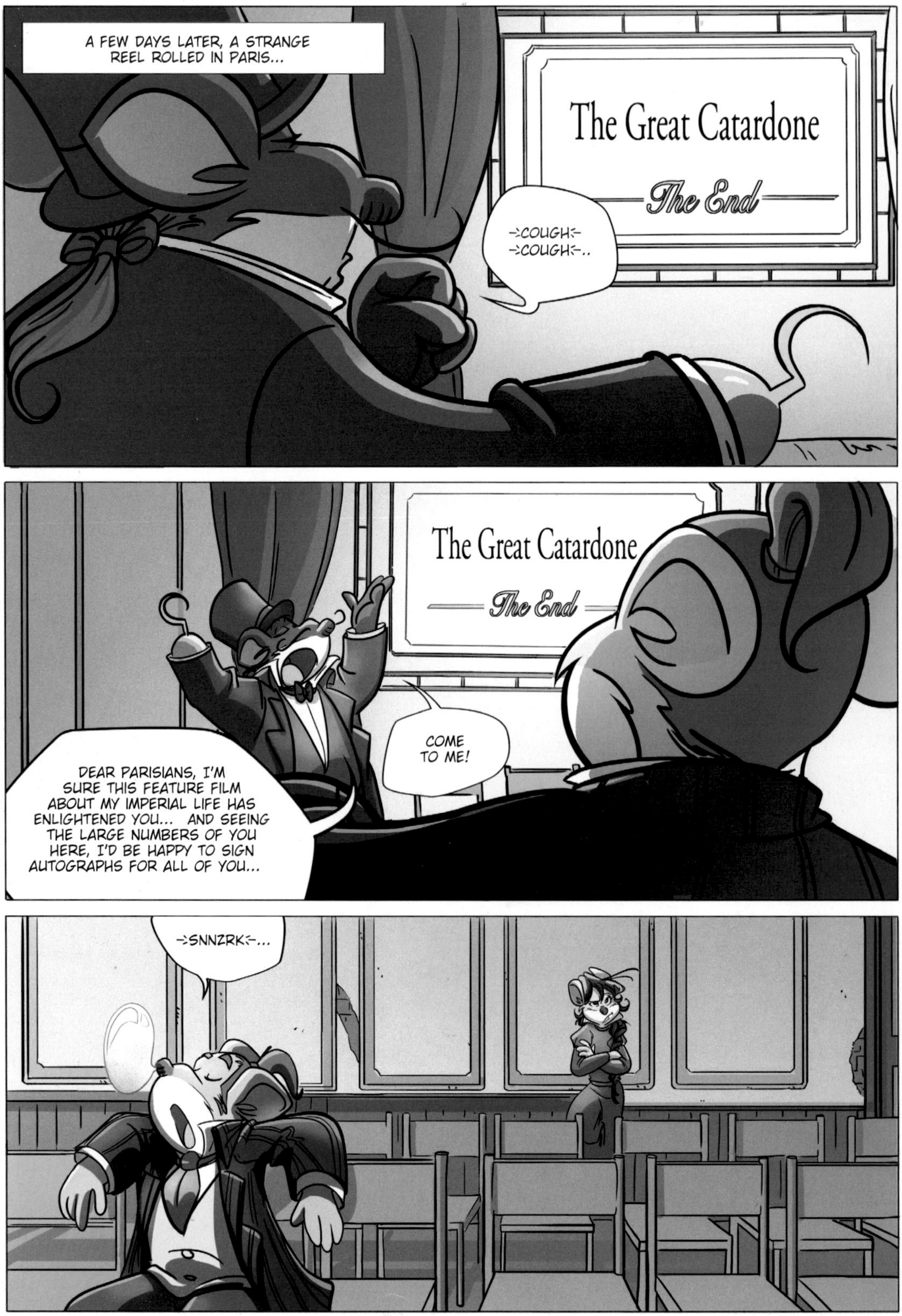
A FEW DAYS LATER, A STRANGE REEL ROLLED IN PARIS...
The Great Catardone
The End
-COUGH- -COUGH-..
The Great Catardone
The End
COME TO ME!
DEAR PARISIANS, I'M SURE THIS FEATURE FILM ABOUT MY IMPERIAL LIFE HAS ENLIGHTENED YOU... AND SEEING THE LARGE NUMBERS OF YOU HERE, I'D BE HAPPY TO SIGN AUTOGRAPHS FOR ALL OF YOU...
-SNNZRK-...

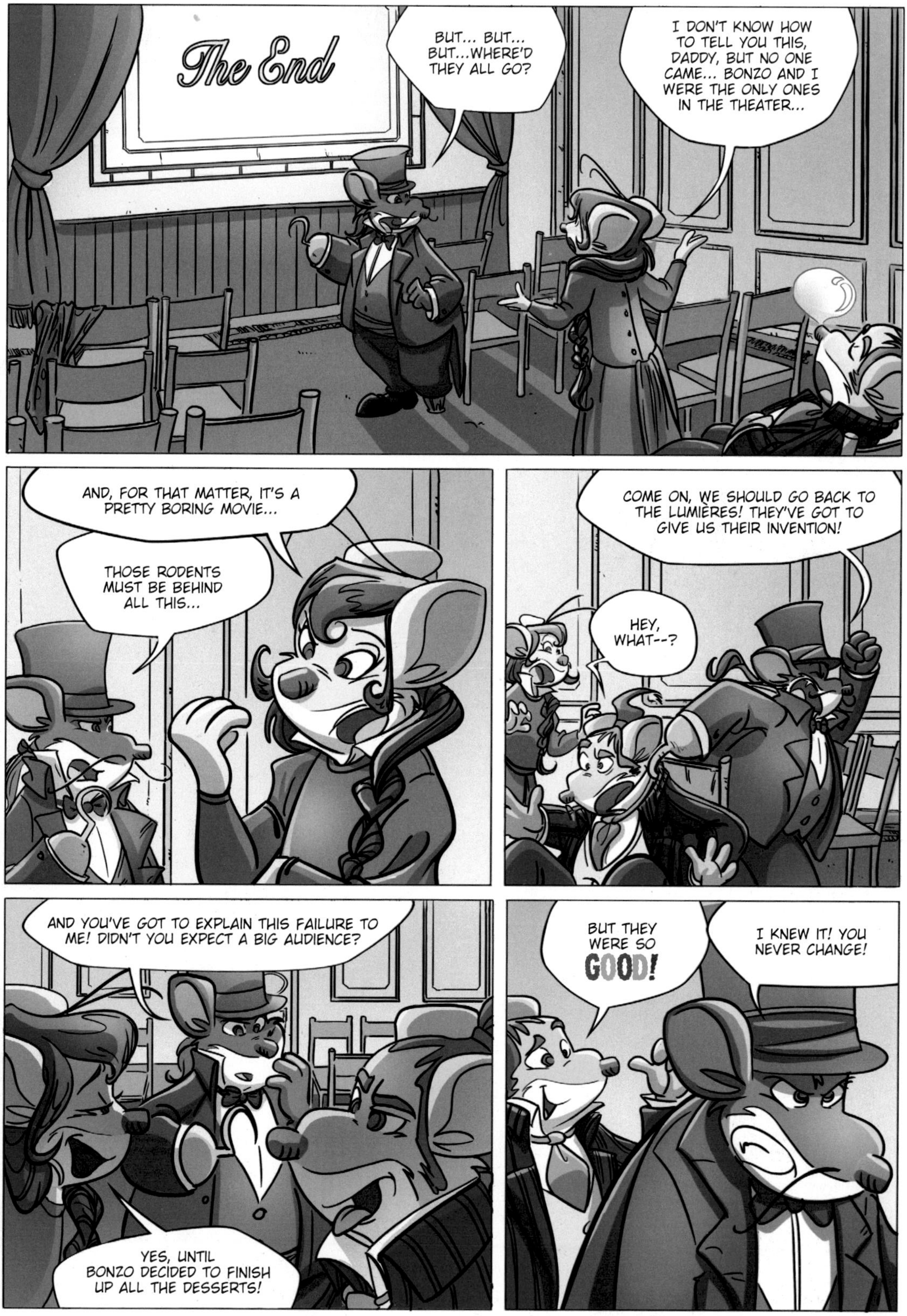
The End
BUT... BUT... BUT...WHERE'D THEY ALL GO?
I DON'T KNOW HOW TO TELL YOU THIS, DADDY, BUT NO ONE CAME... BONZO AND I WERE THE ONLY ONES IN THE THEATER...
AND, FOR THAT MATTER, IT'S A PRETTY BORING MOVIE...
THOSE RODENTS MUST BE BEHIND ALL THIS...
COME ON, WE SHOULD GO BACK TO THE LUMIÈRES! THEY'VE GOT TO GIVE US THEIR INVENTION!
HEY, WHAT--?
AND YOU'VE GOT TO EXPLAIN THIS FAILURE TO ME! DIDN'T YOU EXPECT A BIG AUDIENCE?
YES, UNTIL BONZO DECIDED TO FINISH UP ALL THE DESSERTS!
BUT THEY WERE SO GOOD!
I KNEW IT! YOU NEVER CHANGE!

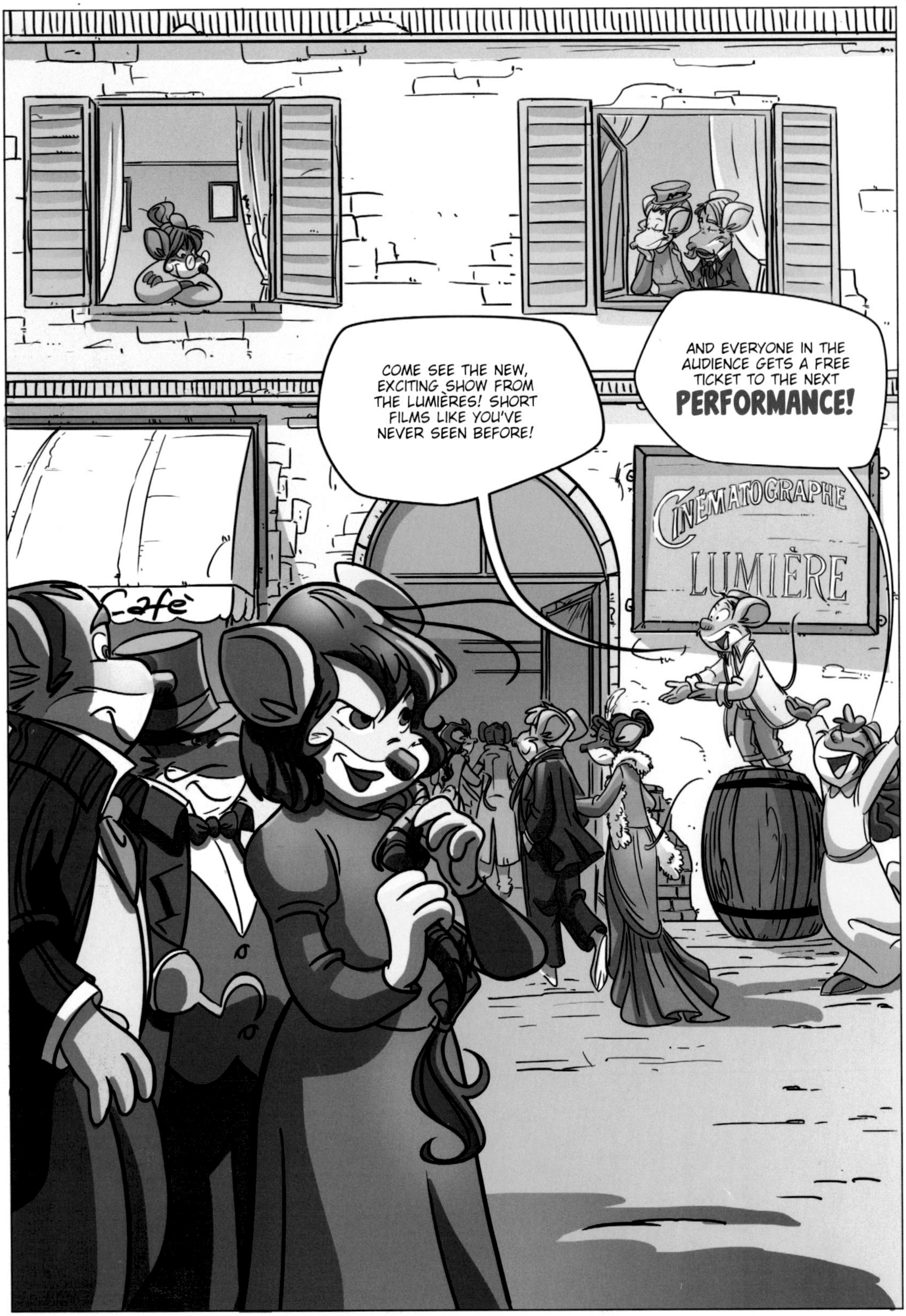

COME SEE THE NEW, EXCITING SHOW FROM THE LUMIÈRES! SHORT FILMS LIKE YOU'VE NEVER SEEN BEFORE!
AND EVERYONE IN THE AUDIENCE GETS A FREE TICKET TO THE NEXT PERFORMANCE!
CINÉMATOGRAPHE LUMIÈRE
Cafè

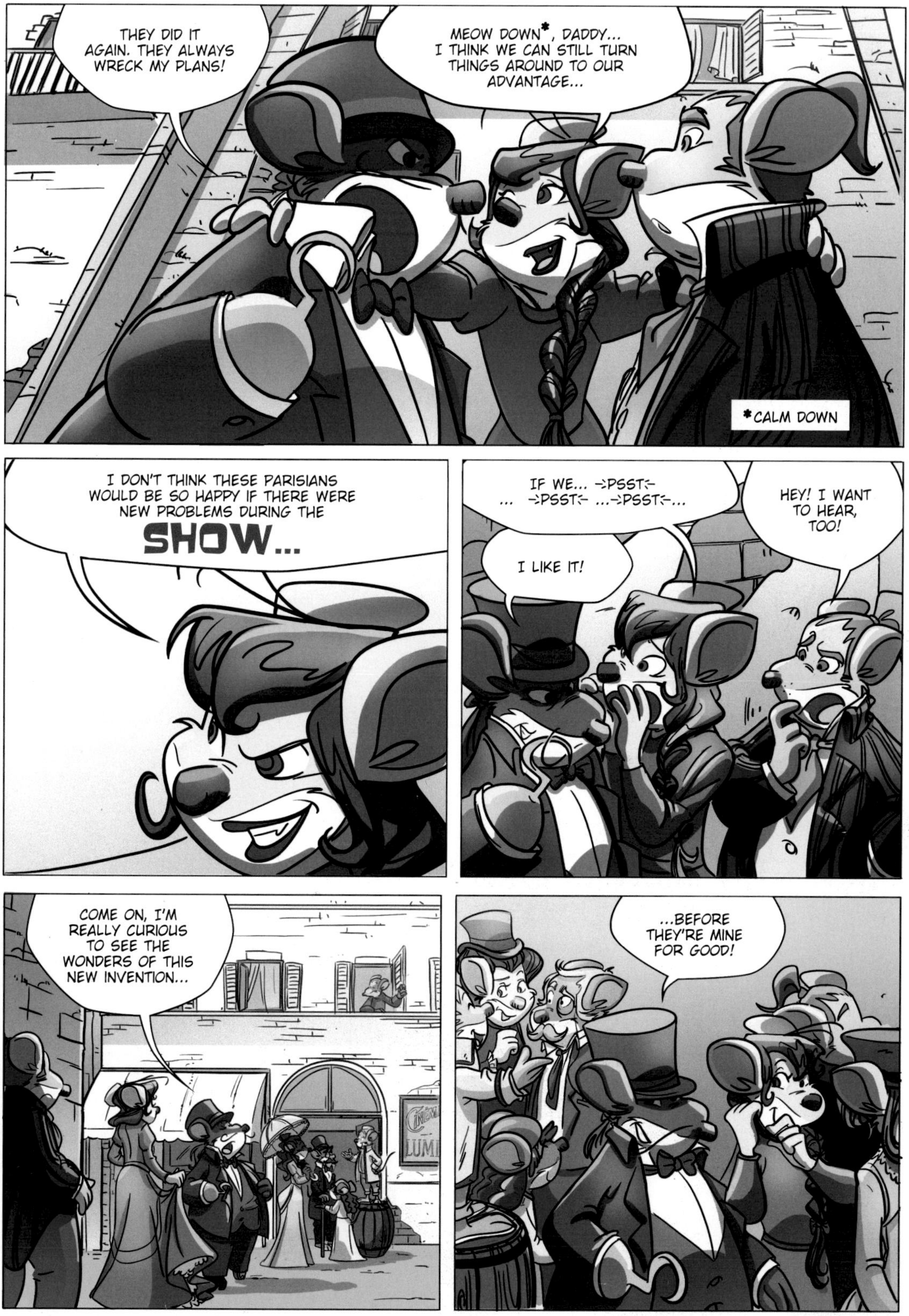
THEY DID IT AGAIN. THEY ALWAYS WRECK MY PLANS!
MEOW DOWN*, DADDY... I THINK WE CAN STILL TURN THINGS AROUND TO OUR ADVANTAGE...
*CALM DOWN
I DON'T THINK THESE PARISIANS WOULD BE SO HAPPY IF THERE WERE NEW PROBLEMS DURING THE SHOW...
IF WE... ->PSST<- ... ->PSST<- ...->PSST<-...
I LIKE IT!
HEY! I WANT TO HEAR, TOO!
COME ON, I'M REALLY CURIOUS TO SEE THE WONDERS OF THIS NEW INVENTION...
...BEFORE THEY'RE MINE FOR GOOD!

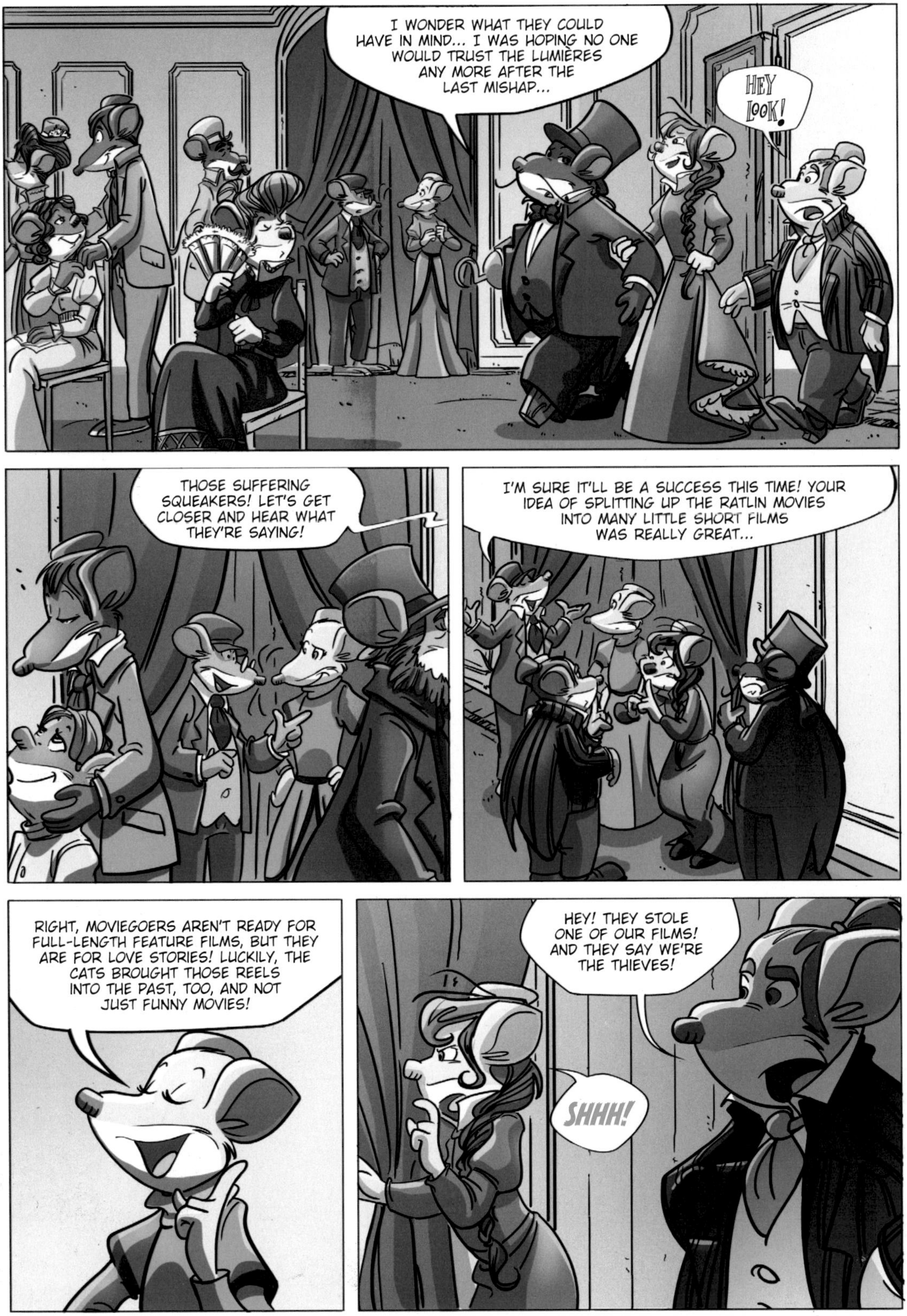
I WONDER WHAT THEY COULD HAVE IN MIND... I WAS HOPING NO ONE WOULD TRUST THE LUMIÈRES ANY MORE AFTER THE LAST MISHAP...
HEY LOOK!
THOSE SUFFERING SQUEAKERS! LET'S GET CLOSER AND HEAR WHAT THEY'RE SAYING!
I'M SURE IT'LL BE A SUCCESS THIS TIME! YOUR IDEA OF SPLITTING UP THE RATLIN MOVIES INTO MANY LITTLE SHORT FILMS WAS REALLY GREAT...
RIGHT, MOVIEGOERS AREN'T READY FOR FULL-LENGTH FEATURE FILMS, BUT THEY ARE FOR LOVE STORIES! LUCKILY, THE CATS BROUGHT THOSE REELS INTO THE PAST, TOO, AND NOT JUST FUNNY MOVIES!
HEY! THEY STOLE ONE OF OUR FILMS! AND THEY SAY WE'RE THE THIEVES!
SHHH!

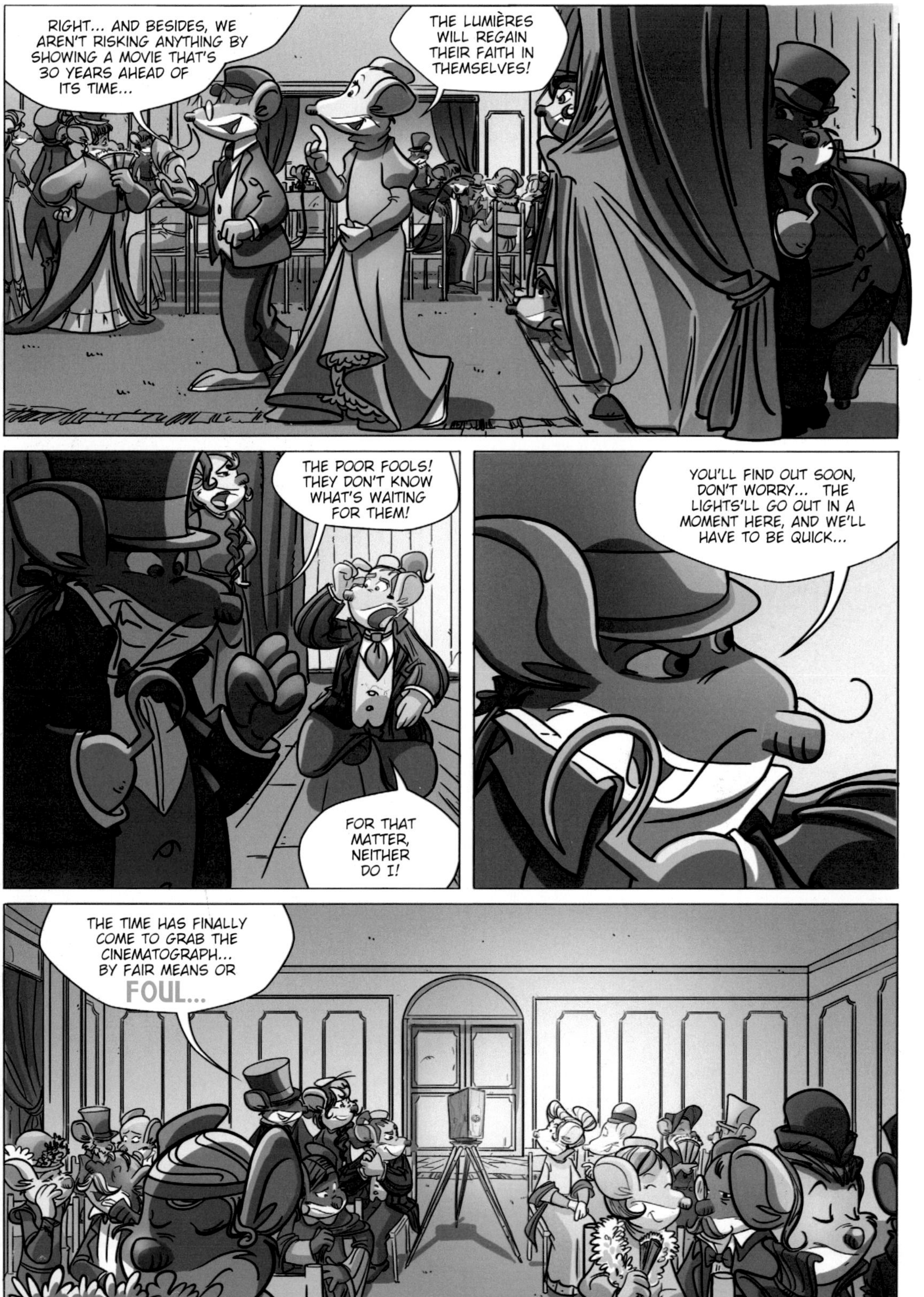
RIGHT... AND BESIDES, WE AREN'T RISKING ANYTHING BY SHOWING A MOVIE THAT'S 30 YEARS AHEAD OF ITS TIME...
THE LUMIÈRES WILL REGAIN THEIR FAITH IN THEMSELVES!
THE POOR FOOLS! THEY DON'T KNOW WHAT'S WAITING FOR THEM!
FOR THAT MATTER, NEITHER DO I!
YOU'LL FIND OUT SOON, DON'T WORRY... THE LIGHTS'LL GO OUT IN A MOMENT HERE, AND WE'LL HAVE TO BE QUICK...
THE TIME HAS FINALLY COME TO GRAB THE CINEMATOGRAPH... BY FAIR MEANS OR FOUL...

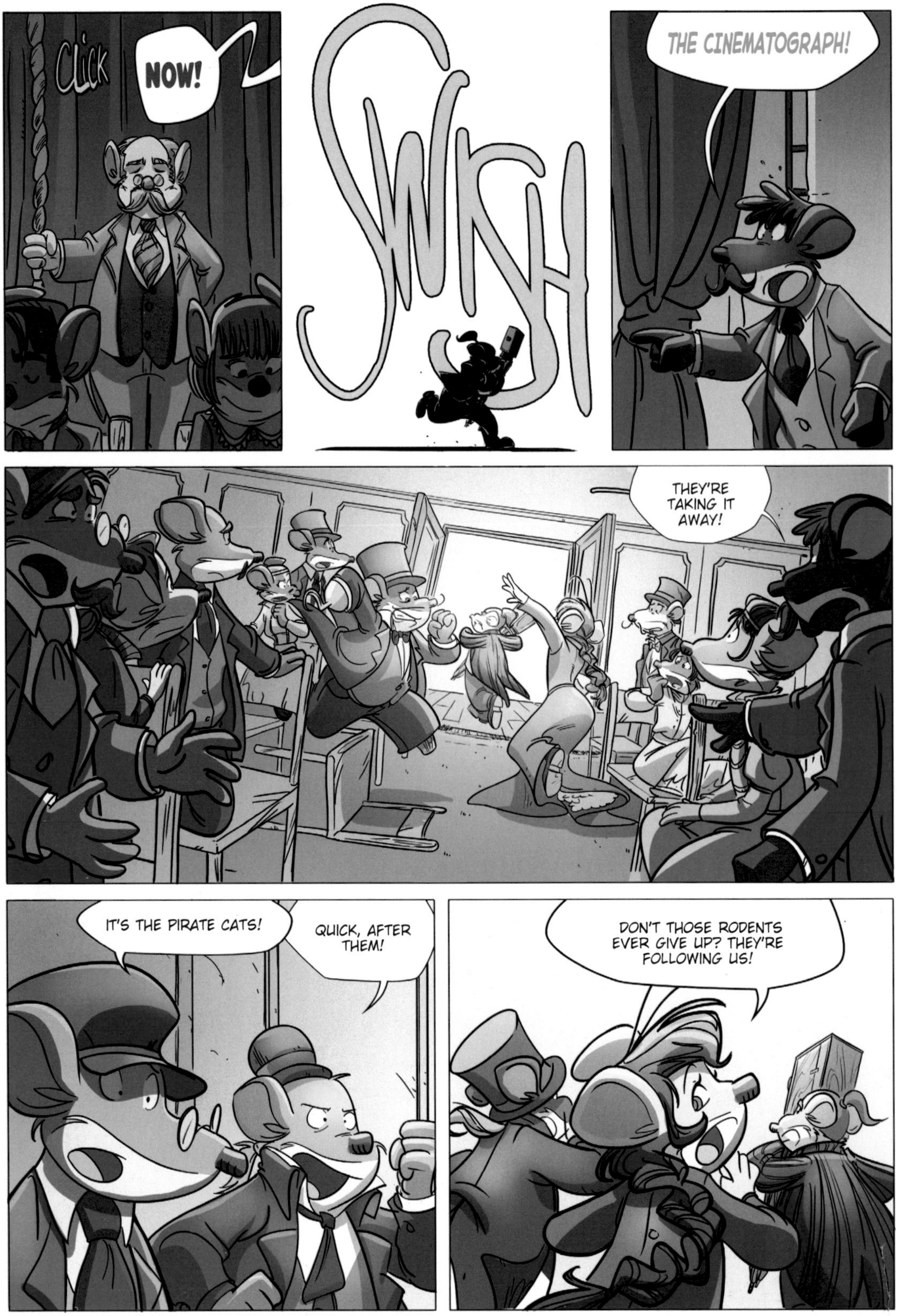
CLICK
NOW!
SWISH
THE CINEMATOGRAPH!
THEY'RE TAKING IT AWAY!
IT'S THE PIRATE CATS!
QUICK, AFTER THEM!
DON'T THOSE RODENTS EVER GIVE UP? THEY'RE FOLLOWING US!

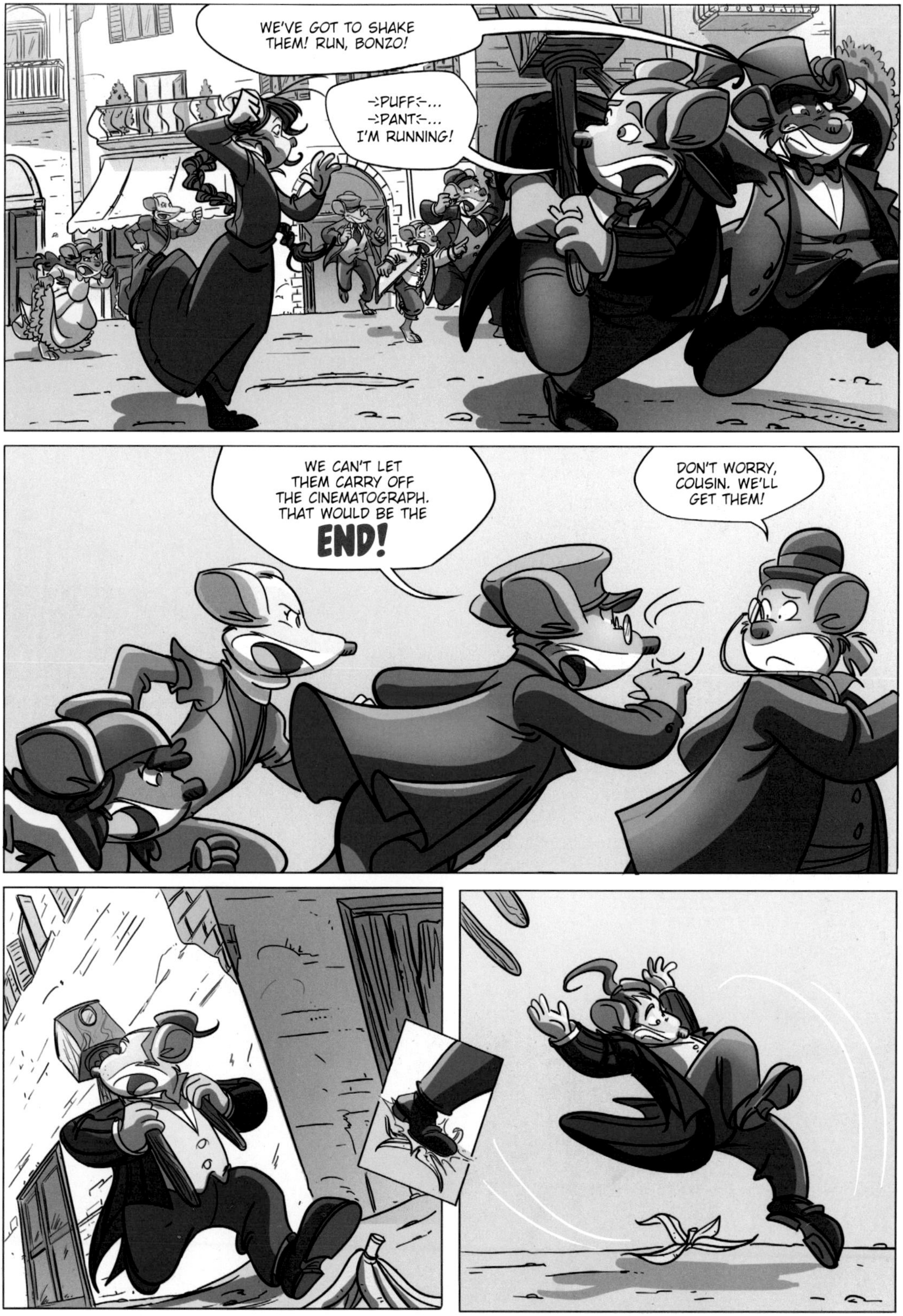
WE'VE GOT TO SHAKE THEM! RUN, BONZO!
-PUFF-... -PANT-... I'M RUNNING!
WE CAN'T LET THEM CARRY OFF THE CINEMATOGRAPH. THAT WOULD BE THE END!
DON'T WORRY, COUSIN. WE'LL GET THEM!

THE CINEMATOGRAPH!

MINE!

DID YOU GET IT?

LOOK OUT, DADDY!

WHY, WHAT--

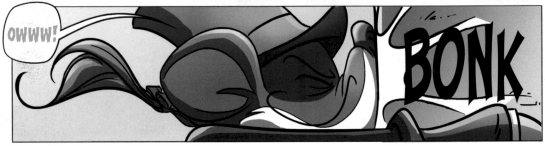

OWWW!

BONK

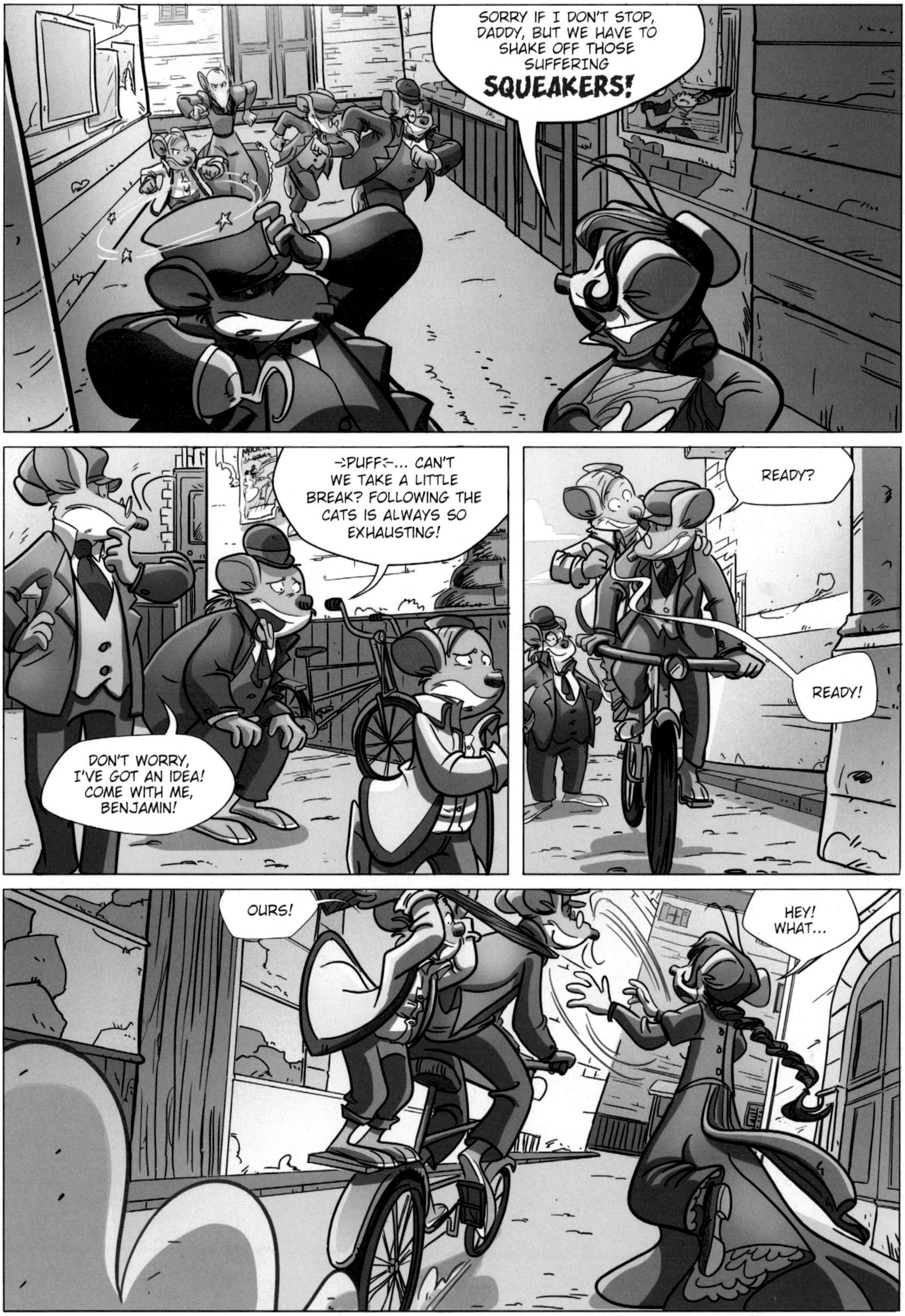
SORRY IF I DON'T STOP, DADDY, BUT WE HAVE TO SHAKE OFF THOSE SUFFERING SQUEAKERS!
-PUFF-... CAN'T WE TAKE A LITTLE BREAK? FOLLOWING THE CATS IS ALWAYS SO EXHAUSTING!
DON'T WORRY, I'VE GOT AN IDEA! COME WITH ME, BENJAMIN!
READY?
READY!
OURS!
HEY! WHAT...

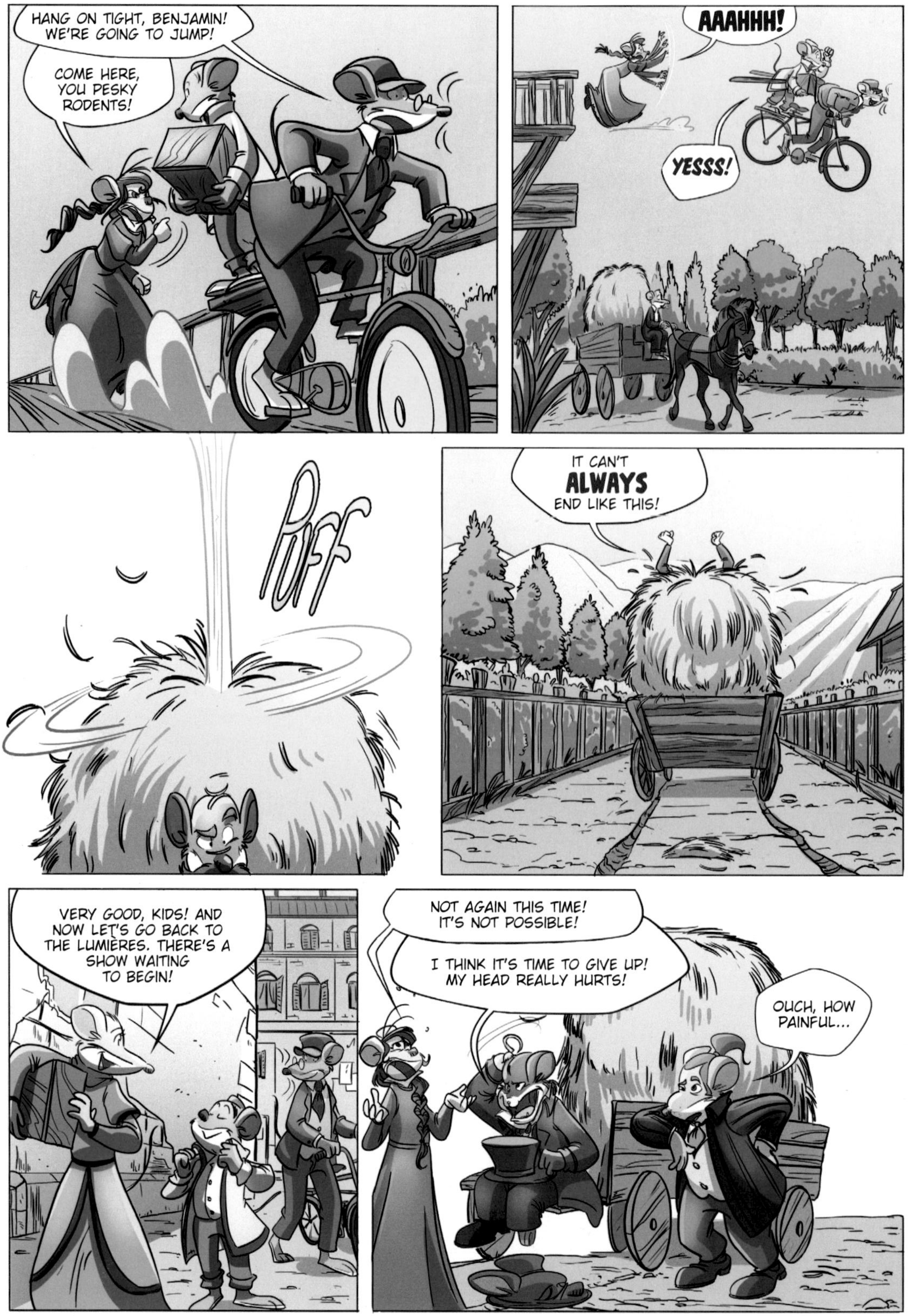
HANG ON TIGHT, BENJAMIN! WE'RE GOING TO JUMP!
COME HERE, YOU PESKY RODENTS!
AAAHHH!
YESSS!
PUFF
IT CAN'T ALWAYS END LIKE THIS!
VERY GOOD, KIDS! AND NOW LET'S GO BACK TO THE LUMIÈRES. THERE'S A SHOW WAITING TO BEGIN!
NOT AGAIN THIS TIME! IT'S NOT POSSIBLE!
I THINK IT'S TIME TO GIVE UP! MY HEAD REALLY HURTS!
OUCH, HOW PAINFUL...

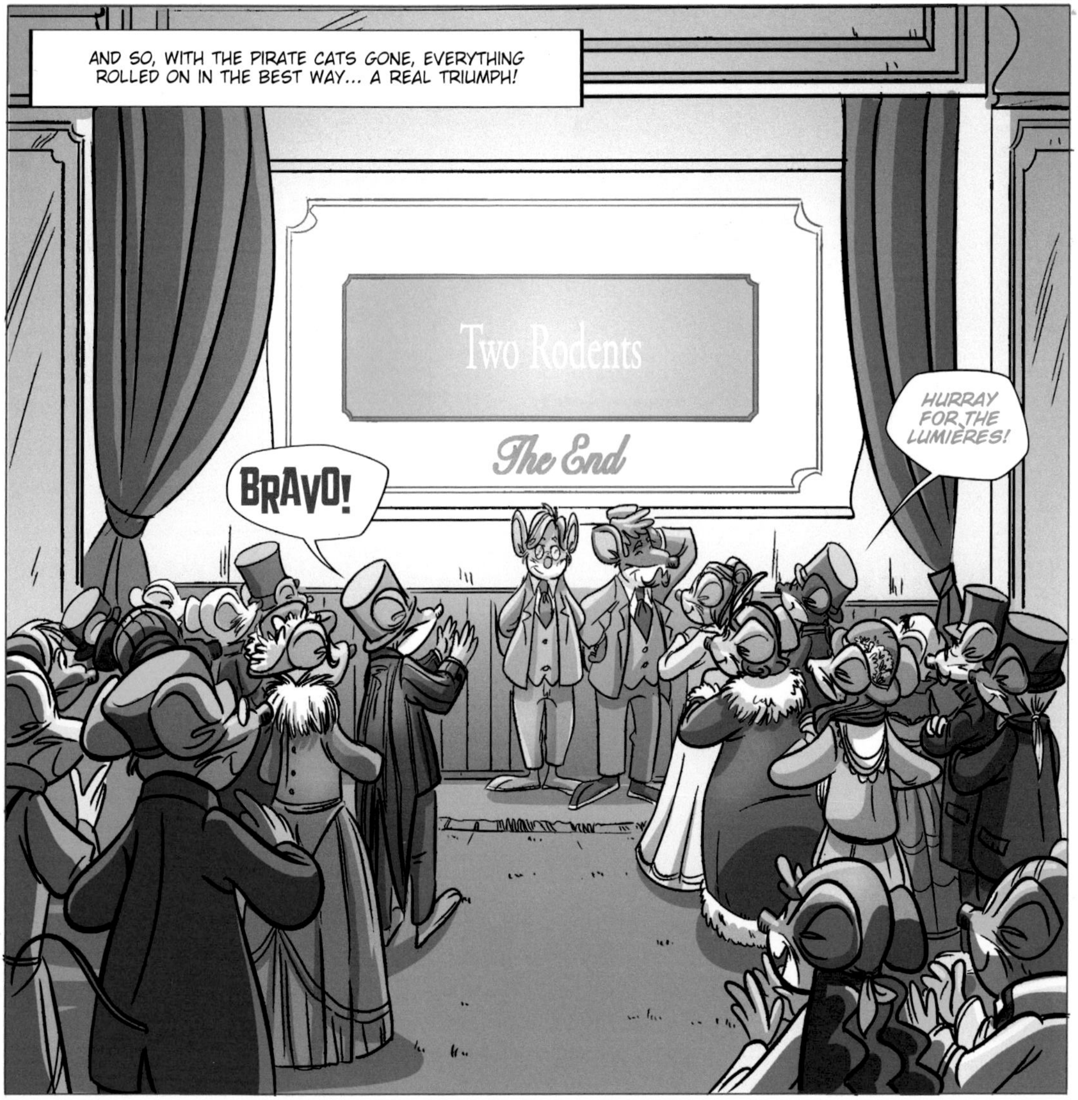
AND SO, WITH THE PIRATE CATS GONE, EVERYTHING ROLLED ON IN THE BEST WAY... A REAL TRIUMPH!
Two Rodents
The End
BRAVO!
HURRAY FOR THE LUMIÈRES!

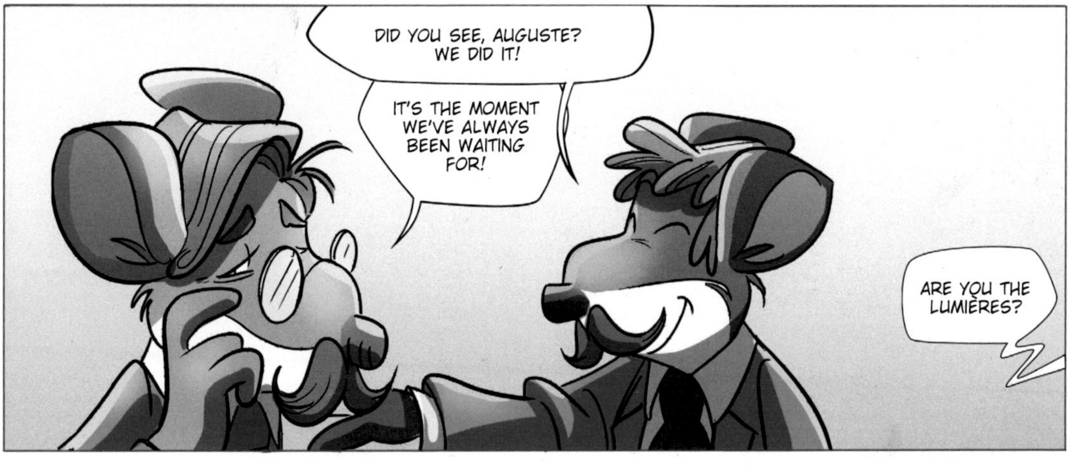
DID YOU SEE, AUGUSTE? WE DID IT!
IT'S THE MOMENT WE'VE ALWAYS BEEN WAITING FOR!
ARE YOU THE LUMIÈRES?

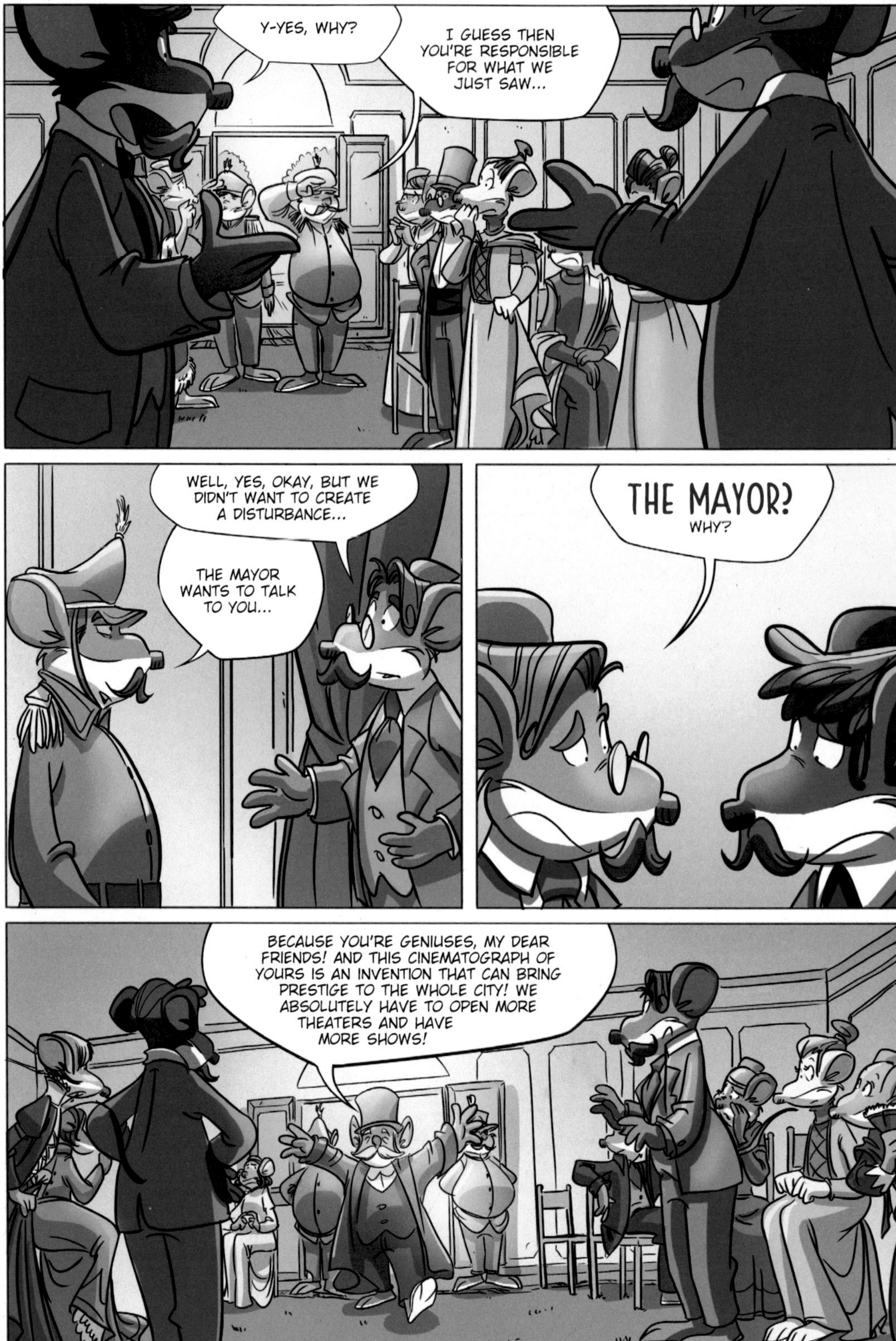
Y-YES, WHY?
I GUESS THEN YOU'RE RESPONSIBLE FOR WHAT WE JUST SAW...
WELL, YES, OKAY, BUT WE DIDN'T WANT TO CREATE A DISTURBANCE...
THE MAYOR WANTS TO TALK TO YOU...
THE MAYOR? WHY?
BECAUSE YOU'RE GENIUSES, MY DEAR FRIENDS! AND THIS CINEMATOGRAPH OF YOURS IS AN INVENTION THAT CAN BRING PRESTIGE TO THE WHOLE CITY! WE ABSOLUTELY HAVE TO OPEN MORE THEATERS AND HAVE MORE SHOWS!

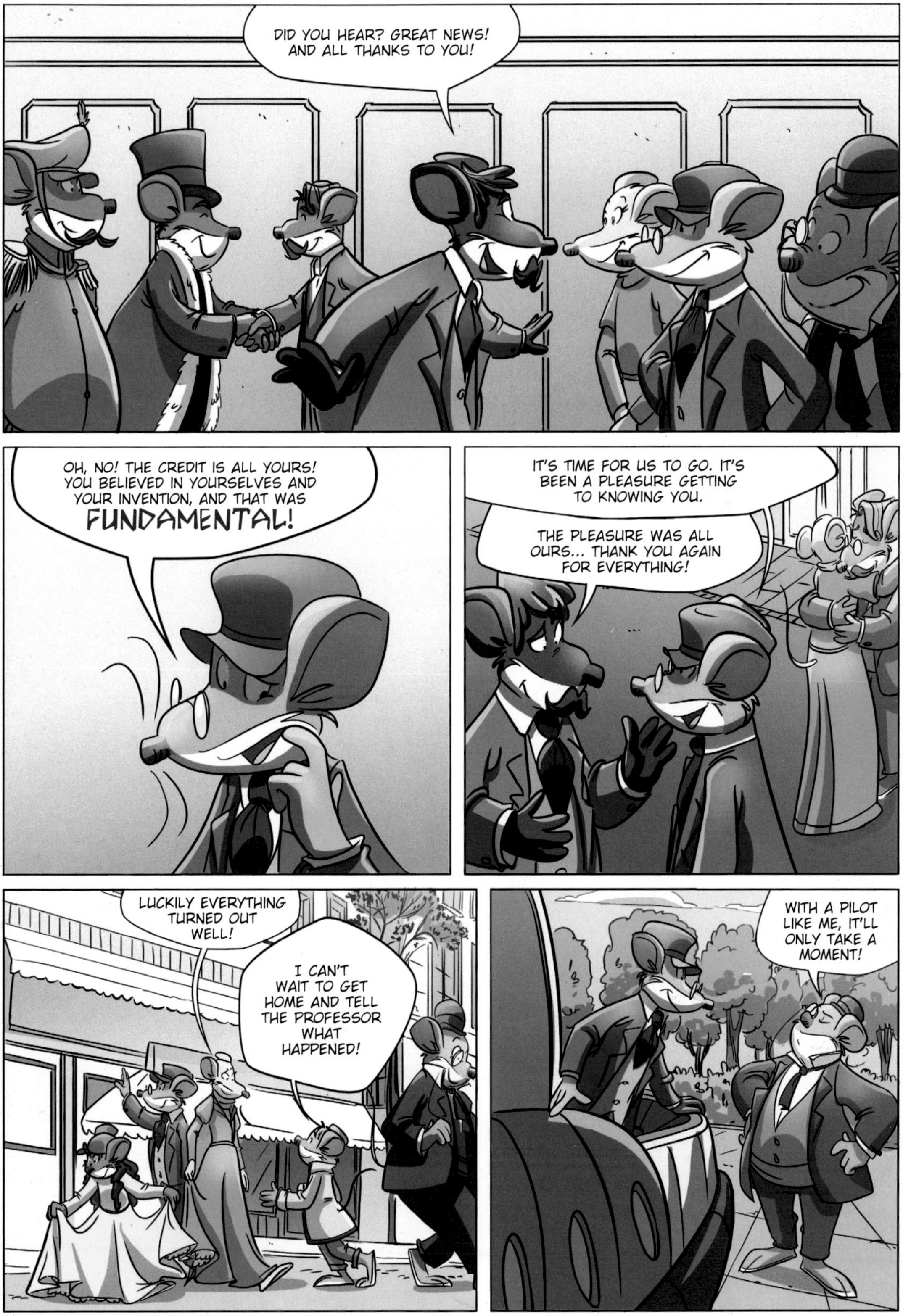
DID YOU HEAR? GREAT NEWS! AND ALL THANKS TO YOU!
OH, NO! THE CREDIT IS ALL YOURS! YOU BELIEVED IN YOURSELVES AND YOUR INVENTION, AND THAT WAS FUNDAMENTAL!
IT'S TIME FOR US TO GO. IT'S BEEN A PLEASURE GETTING TO KNOWING YOU.
THE PLEASURE WAS ALL OURS... THANK YOU AGAIN FOR EVERYTHING!
LUCKILY EVERYTHING TURNED OUT WELL!
I CAN'T WAIT TO GET HOME AND TELL THE PROFESSOR WHAT HAPPENED!
WITH A PILOT LIKE ME, IT'LL ONLY TAKE A MOMENT!

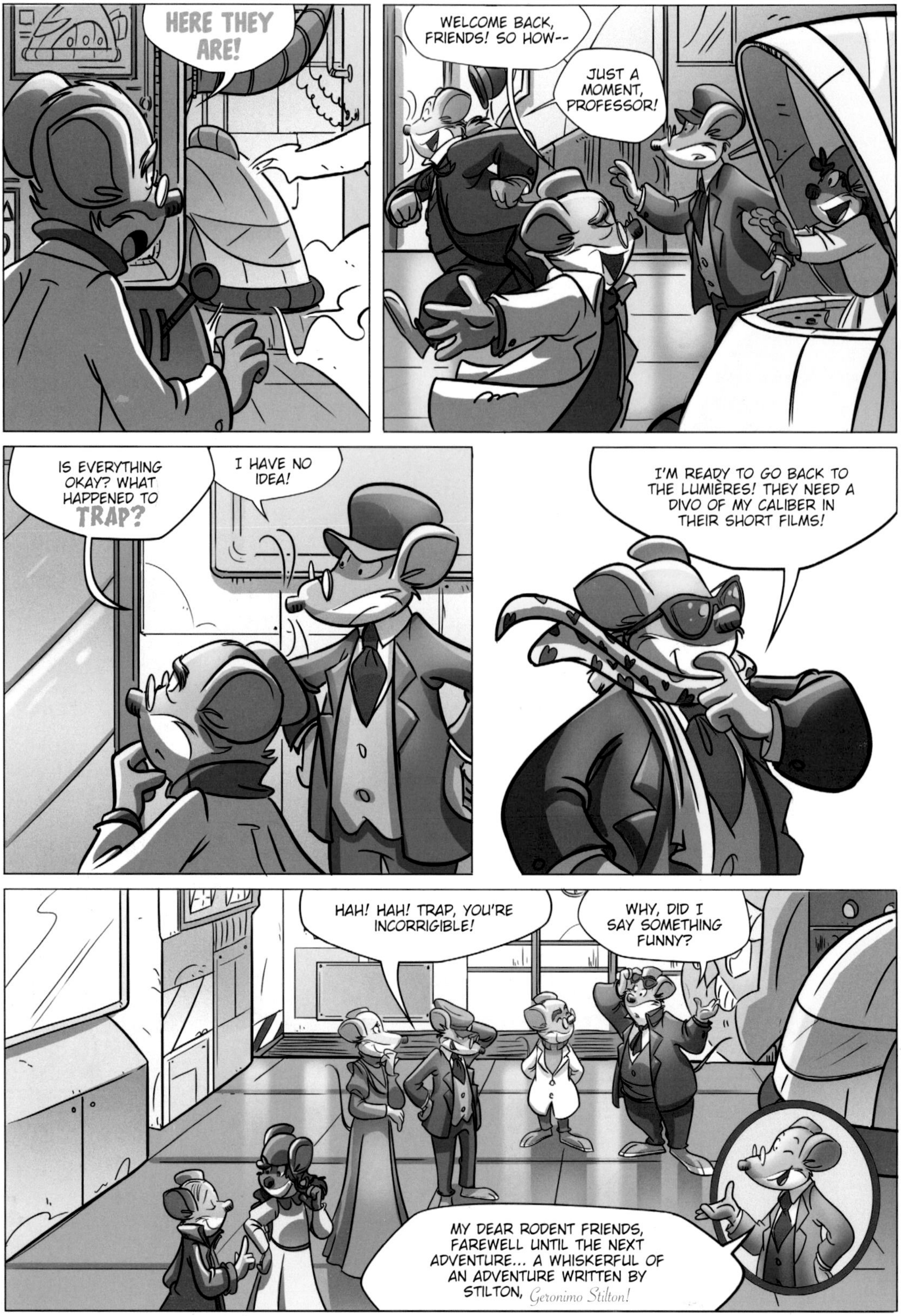
HERE THEY ARE!
WELCOME BACK, FRIENDS! SO HOW--
JUST A MOMENT, PROFESSOR!
IS EVERYTHING OKAY? WHAT HAPPENED TO TRAP?
I HAVE NO IDEA!
I'M READY TO GO BACK TO THE LUMIÈRES! THEY NEED A DIVO OF MY CALIBER IN THEIR SHORT FILMS!
HAH! HAH! TRAP, YOU'RE INCORRIGIBLE!
WHY, DID I SAY SOMETHING FUNNY?
MY DEAR RODENT FRIENDS, FAREWELL UNTIL THE NEXT ADVENTURE... A WHISKERFUL OF AN ADVENTURE WRITTEN BY STILTON, Geronimo Stilton!

Watch Out For PAPERCUTZ™

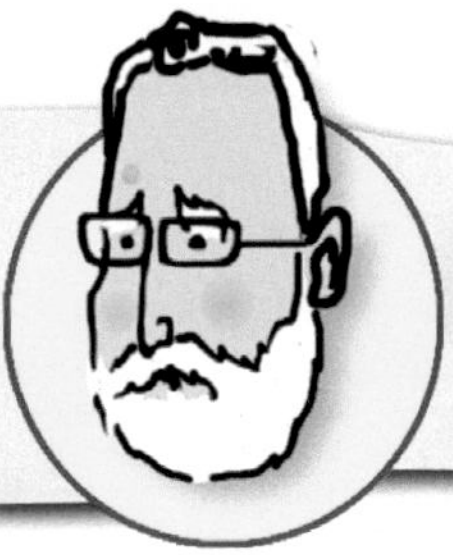

Welcome to the cinematic, sixteenth GERONIMO STILTON graphic novel from Papercutz, those manic moviegoers dedicated to publishing great graphic novels for all ages. I'm Salicrup, *Jim Salicrup*, the Editor-in-Chief and proud IMDB listee. If you haven't already experienced this graphic novel's feature attraction, may I suggest you do so with a bag of popcorn?

Gee, seems like we just visited France in our last GERONIMO STILTON graphic novel-- #15 "All for Stilton, Stilton for All!" In fact, we did! And as the title of GERONIMO STILTON #11 suggests, "We'll Always Have Paris."

I really have to thank good ol' Geronimo—not only did he save the printing press from the clutches of the Pirate Cats (in GERONIMO STILTON #9 "The Weird Book Machine"), thus saving my job as Editor-in-Chief of Papercutz (a book publisher!), but now he's rescued movies as well! I hate to think what film would be like if Catardone III of Catatonia were in charge. As if the heads of Hollywood studios weren't crazy enough, we don't need the head of the Pirate Cats calling the shots—literally! It would be a cat-tastrophe!

Fortunately for all of us, Professor Von Volt keeps an eye on things, and whenever those darn cats try to cause any trouble, he's there to sic Geronimo & Company on them. Of course this means Geronimo can't even see an entire Top Direction concert without being called away to once again save the world. (A bit of Salicrup trivia: if you look very, very closely at the movie poster for the One Direction concert movie, I'm one of the gazillion fans in the background!)

While I tend to always think of GERONIMO STILTON graphic novels as really exciting adventure stories, featuring some really fun characters, I sometimes forget that each one is loaded with lots of fun-facts. If you're not careful, you might actually learn something here. Take me, for example. I would've bet anything that Thomas Edison was the inventor of motion pictures. At least that's what I remember being taught in school. Turns out, as we discover on page 28, "Before the Lumières, devices like the CINEMATOGRAPH had already been invented. Thomas Edison had created the 'kinetiscope,' which could not, however, project the images. In France, Étienne-Jules Marey had invented the 'chronophotograph.' But it turned out to be too complicated." So, it was the Lumière brothers who provided the finishing touches that made motion pictures possible (And anyone who ever watched Disney's *Beauty and the Beast* knows, "lumière" is the French word for light! How cool is it that the name of the brothers who created the movie projector, which is a device that projects light, through film, onto a screen, means "light"? Hey, who says this page can't be educational too?!)

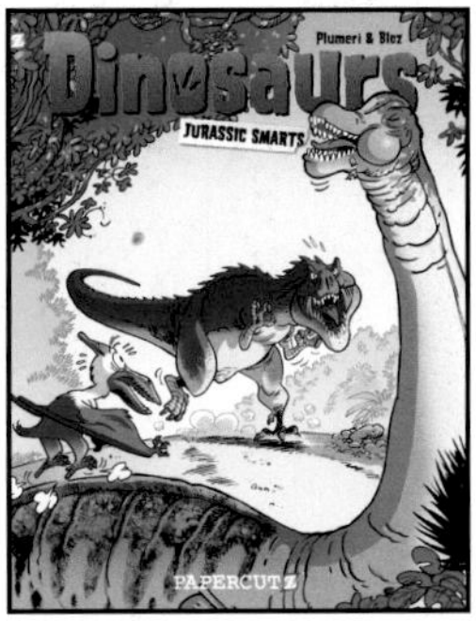
Plumeri & Bloz
Dinosaurs
JURASSIC SMARTS
PAPERCUTZ

And speaking of educational and fun, have we mentioned the hit Papercutz graphic novel series DINOSAURS lately? If you enjoyed GERONIMO STILTON #5 ("The Great Ice Age") or #7 ("Dinosaurs in Action"), you're going to love DINOSAURS by Arnaud Plumeri, writer, and Bloz, artist. Paleontologist Indino Jones has great fun telling us all about the latest dino-discoveries. Check out the preview of DINOSAURS #3 "Jurassic Smarts" that starts on the very next page.

Of course, you won't want to miss the next exciting Geronimo Stilton adventure either! We have a Big Announcement to make in GERONIMO STILTON #17, but let me warn you in advance that we'll be changing the look of the covers of this series starting with #17, so be sure to look carefully! But don't worry-- one thing that will not change is that our favorite Editor of The Rodent's Gazette will again save the future, by protecting the past!

Jim

STAY IN TOUCH!

EMAIL:	salicrup@papercutz.com
WEB:	papercutz.com
TWITTER:	@papercutzgn
FACEBOOK:	PAPERCUTZGRAPHICNOVELS
FAN MAIL:	Papercutz, 160 Broadway, Suite 700, East Wing, New York, NY 10038

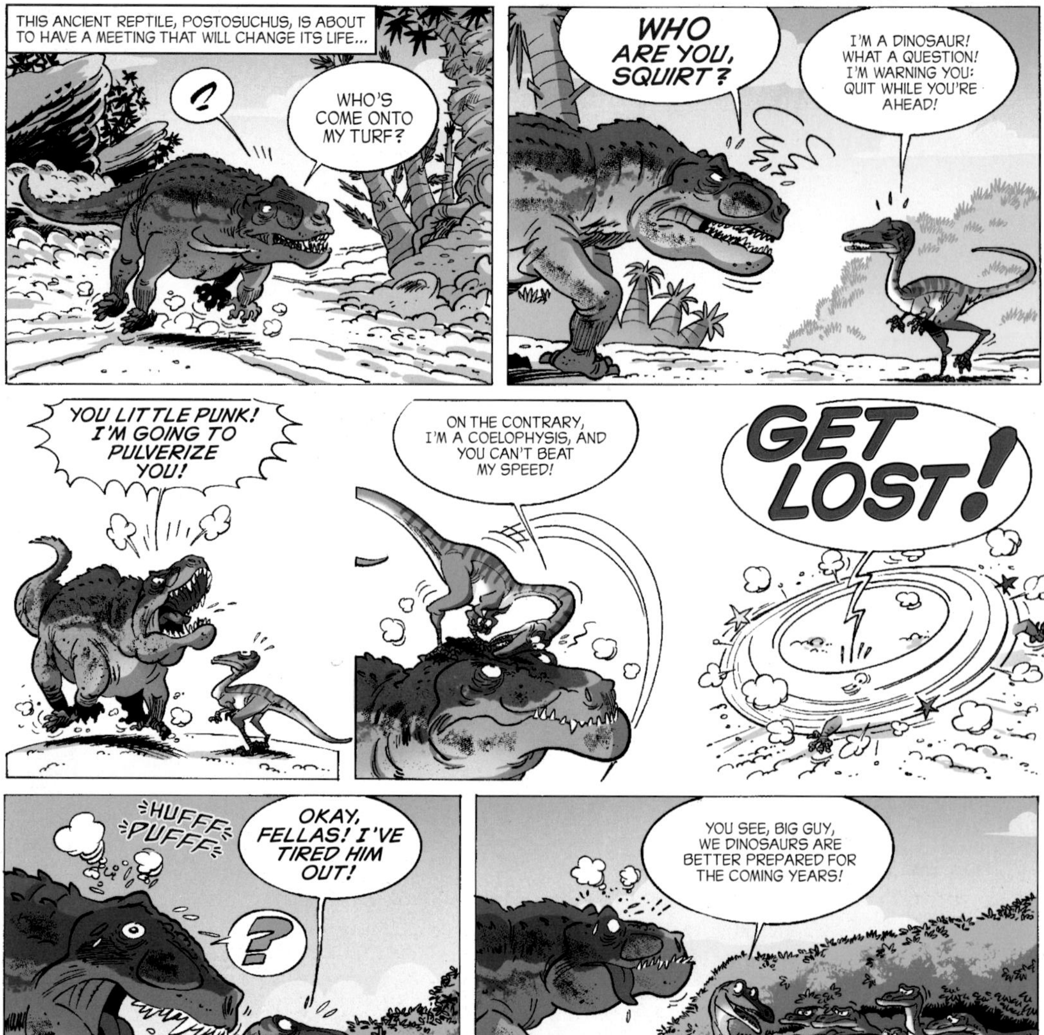
THIS ANCIENT REPTILE, POSTOSUCHUS, IS ABOUT TO HAVE A MEETING THAT WILL CHANGE ITS LIFE...
?
WHO'S COME ONTO MY TURF?
WHO ARE YOU, SQUIRT?
I'M A DINOSAUR! WHAT A QUESTION! I'M WARNING YOU: QUIT WHILE YOU'RE AHEAD!
YOU LITTLE PUNK! I'M GOING TO PULVERIZE YOU!
ON THE CONTRARY, I'M A COELOPHYSIS, AND YOU CAN'T BEAT MY SPEED!
GET LOST!
HUFFF PUFFF
OKAY, FELLAS! I'VE TIRED HIM OUT!
?
YOU SEE, BIG GUY, WE DINOSAURS ARE BETTER PREPARED FOR THE COMING YEARS!

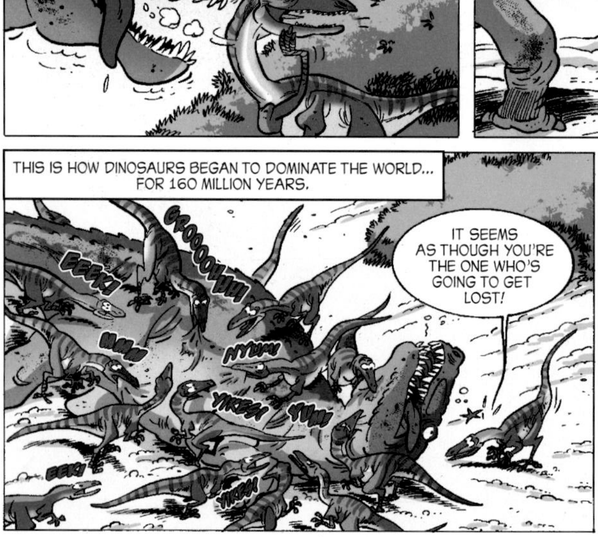
THIS IS HOW DINOSAURS BEGAN TO DOMINATE THE WORLD... FOR 160 MILLION YEARS.
GROOOOOWHH
EEEK!
IT SEEMS AS THOUGH YOU'RE THE ONE WHO'S GOING TO GET LOST!
YIKES!
EEEK!

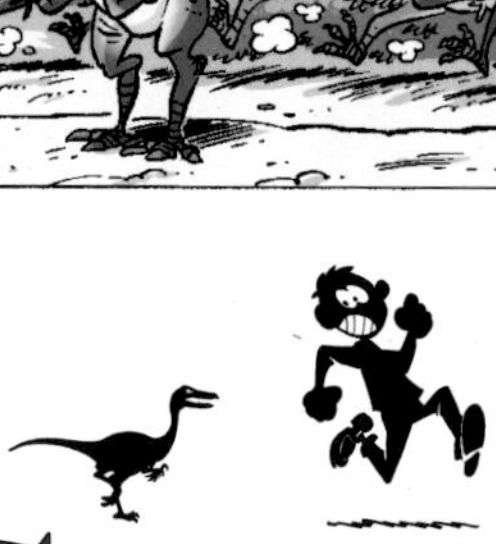

COELOPHYSIS

MEANING: HOLLOW FORM
PERIOD: LATE TRIASSIC (228 TO 203 MILLION YEARS AGO)
ORDER/ FAMILY: SAURISCHIA/ COELOPHYSIDAE
SIZE: 8 FEET LONG
WEIGHT: 65 POUNDS
DIET: CARNIVORE
FOUND: UNITED STATES

PLUMERI & BLOZ

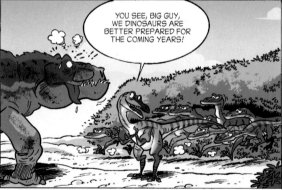

DINNER'S READY!

SWEET! WHAT ARE WE HAVING, BOSS?

NECK!

WHAT?! AGAIN?

WELL, YES! NECK, NECK, AND NECK!

RRAAA... I CAN'T STAND IT ANY LONGER!

I'M FED UP! THAT MAKES TWO WEEKS NOW WHERE THAT'S ALL WE'VE EATEN!

EVEN FOR DESSERT!

YUCK

WELL, YEAH, SMART ALECK! BUT I ALREADY TOLD YOU...

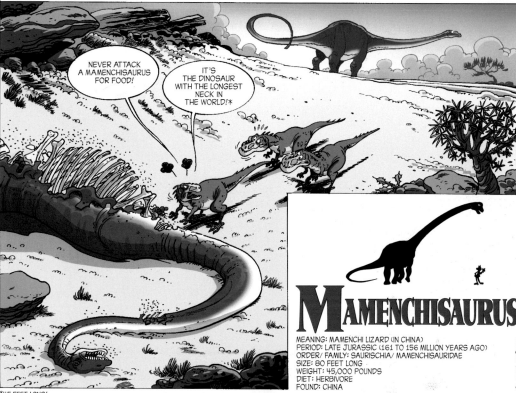

NEVER ATTACK A MAMENCHISAURUS FOR FOOD!

IT'S THE DINOSAUR WITH THE LONGEST NECK IN THE WORLD!*

MAMENCHISAURUS

MEANING: MAMENCHI LIZARD (IN CHINA)
PERIOD: LATE JURASSIC (161 TO 156 MILLION YEARS AGO)
ORDER/ FAMILY: SAURISCHIA/ MAMENCHISAURIDAE
SIZE: 80 FEET LONG
WEIGHT: 45,000 POUNDS
DIET: HERBIVORE
FOUND: CHINA

*45 FEET LONG!

A QUESTION OF WEIGHT

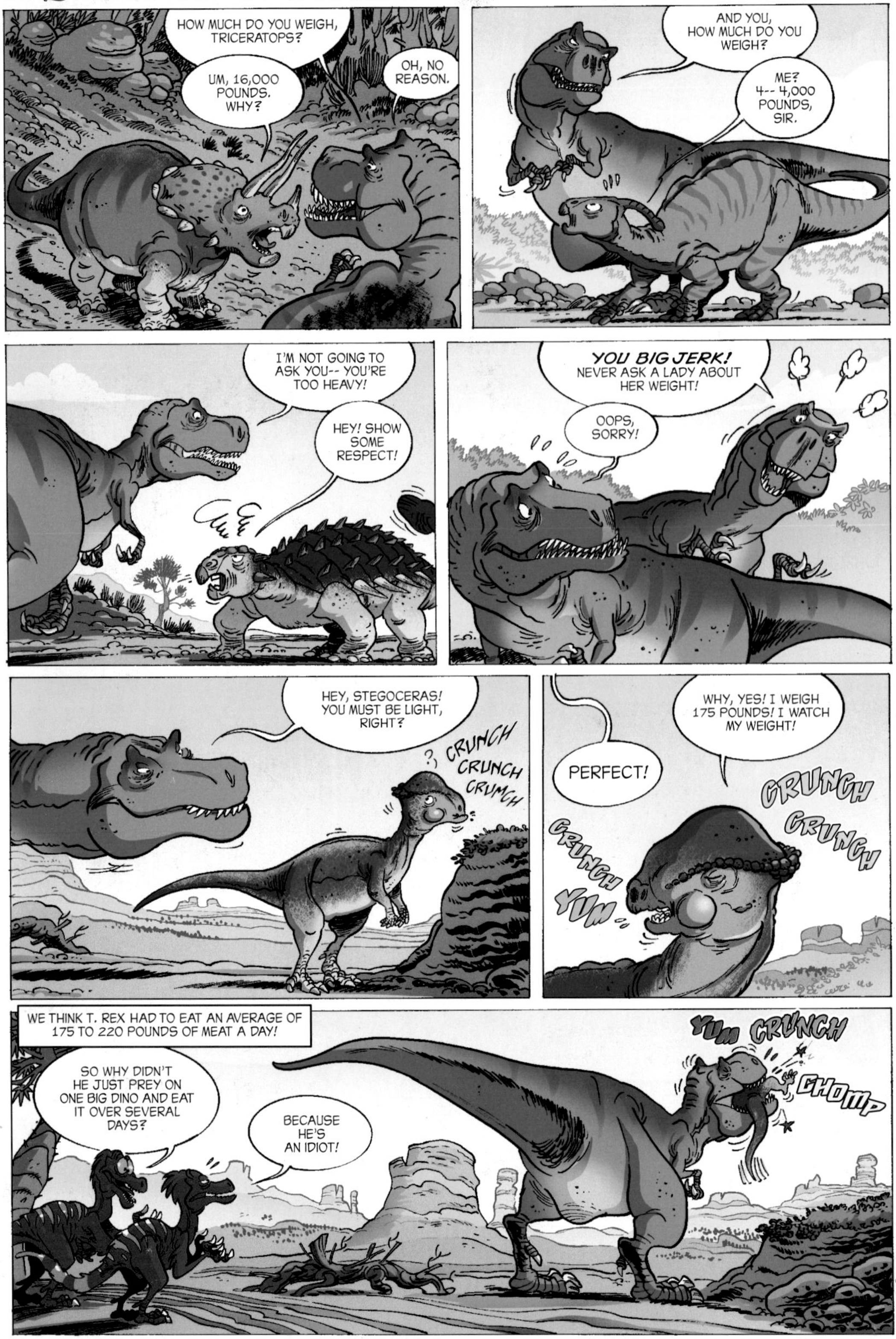

HOW MUCH DO YOU WEIGH, TRICERATOPS?
UM, 16,000 POUNDS. WHY?
OH, NO REASON.
AND YOU, HOW MUCH DO YOU WEIGH?
ME? 4-- 4,000 POUNDS, SIR.
I'M NOT GOING TO ASK YOU-- YOU'RE TOO HEAVY!
HEY! SHOW SOME RESPECT!
YOU BIG JERK! NEVER ASK A LADY ABOUT HER WEIGHT!
OOPS, SORRY!
HEY, STEGOCERAS! YOU MUST BE LIGHT, RIGHT?
CRUNCH CRUNCH CRUNCH
WHY, YES! I WEIGH 175 POUNDS! I WATCH MY WEIGHT!
PERFECT!
CRUNCH CRUNCH CRUNCH YUM
WE THINK T. REX HAD TO EAT AN AVERAGE OF 175 TO 220 POUNDS OF MEAT A DAY!
SO WHY DIDN'T HE JUST PREY ON ONE BIG DINO AND EAT IT OVER SEVERAL DAYS?
BECAUSE HE'S AN IDIOT!
YUM CRUNCH
CHOMP

OVIRAPTOR

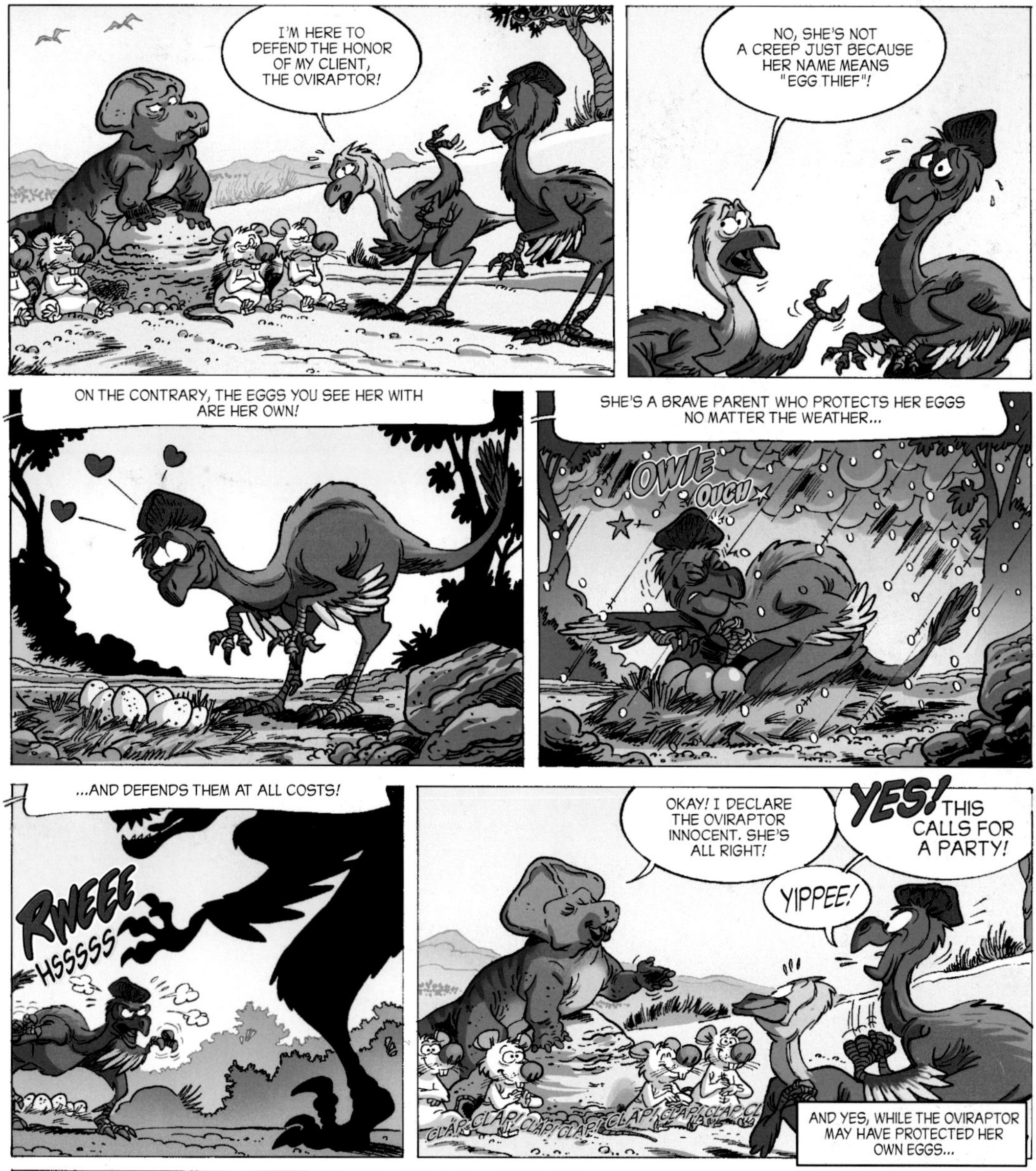

I'M HERE TO DEFEND THE HONOR OF MY CLIENT, THE OVIRAPTOR!
NO, SHE'S NOT A CREEP JUST BECAUSE HER NAME MEANS "EGG THIEF"!
ON THE CONTRARY, THE EGGS YOU SEE HER WITH ARE HER OWN!
SHE'S A BRAVE PARENT WHO PROTECTS HER EGGS NO MATTER THE WEATHER...
OWIE
OUCH
...AND DEFENDS THEM AT ALL COSTS!
RWEEE
HSSSSS
OKAY! I DECLARE THE OVIRAPTOR INNOCENT. SHE'S ALL RIGHT!
YES! THIS CALLS FOR A PARTY!
YIPPEE!
CLAP! CLAP! CLAP! CLAP! CLAP! CLAP! CLAP!
AND YES, WHILE THE OVIRAPTOR MAY HAVE PROTECTED HER OWN EGGS...

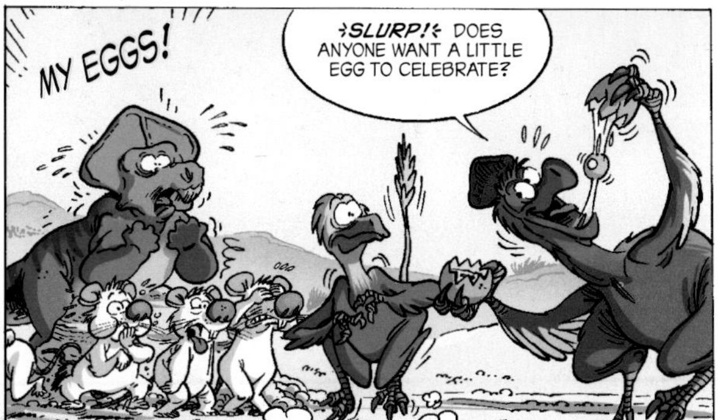

MY EGGS!
SLURP! DOES ANYONE WANT A LITTLE EGG TO CELEBRATE?
...SHE WOULDN'T TURN DOWN SOMEONE ELSE'S!

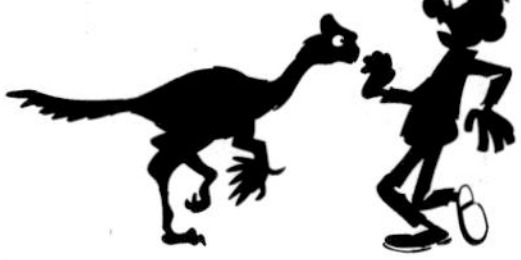

OVIRAPTOR

MEANING: EGG THIEF
PERIOD: LATE CRETACEOUS (85 TO 70 MILLION YEARS AGO)
ORDER/ FAMILY: SAURISCHIA/ OVIRAPTORIDAE
SIZE: 2.5 FEET LONG
WEIGHT: 65 POUNDS
DIET: OMNIVORE?
FOUND: MONGOLIA

PLUMERI & BLOZ

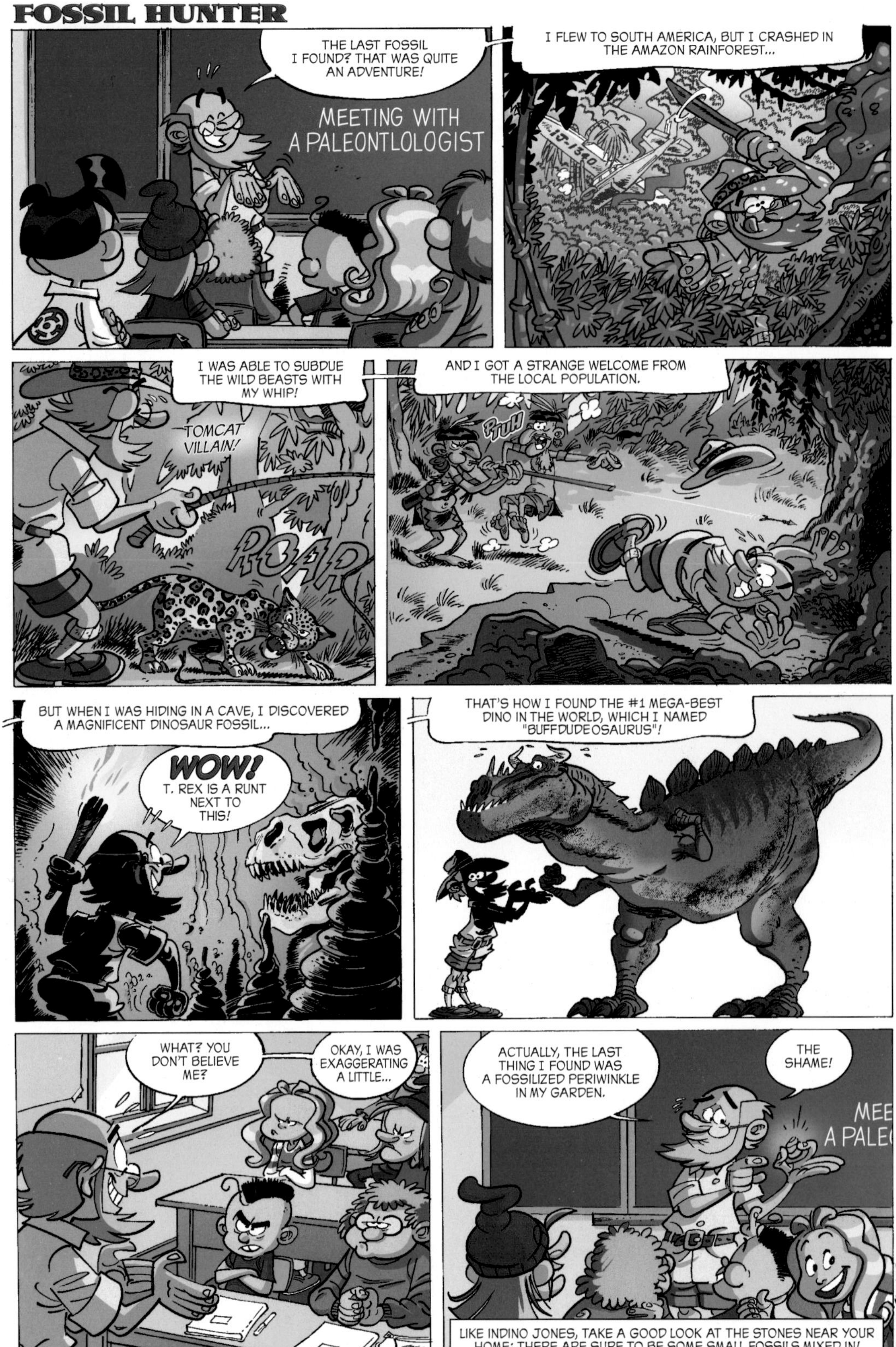
FOSSIL HUNTER
THE LAST FOSSIL I FOUND? THAT WAS QUITE AN ADVENTURE!
MEETING WITH A PALEONTLOLOGIST
I FLEW TO SOUTH AMERICA, BUT I CRASHED IN THE AMAZON RAINFOREST...
I WAS ABLE TO SUBDUE THE WILD BEASTS WITH MY WHIP!
TOMCAT VILLAIN!
ROAR
AND I GOT A STRANGE WELCOME FROM THE LOCAL POPULATION.
PTUH
BUT WHEN I WAS HIDING IN A CAVE, I DISCOVERED A MAGNIFICENT DINOSAUR FOSSIL...
WOW! T. REX IS A RUNT NEXT TO THIS!
THAT'S HOW I FOUND THE #1 MEGA-BEST DINO IN THE WORLD, WHICH I NAMED "BUFFDUDEOSAURUS"!
WHAT? YOU DON'T BELIEVE ME?
OKAY, I WAS EXAGGERATING A LITTLE...
ACTUALLY, THE LAST THING I FOUND WAS A FOSSILIZED PERIWINKLE IN MY GARDEN.
THE SHAME!
LIKE INDINO JONES, TAKE A GOOD LOOK AT THE STONES NEAR YOUR HOME: THERE ARE SURE TO BE SOME SMALL FOSSILS MIXED IN!

Don't miss DINOSAURS #3 "Jurassic Smarts" available at booksellers everywhere!

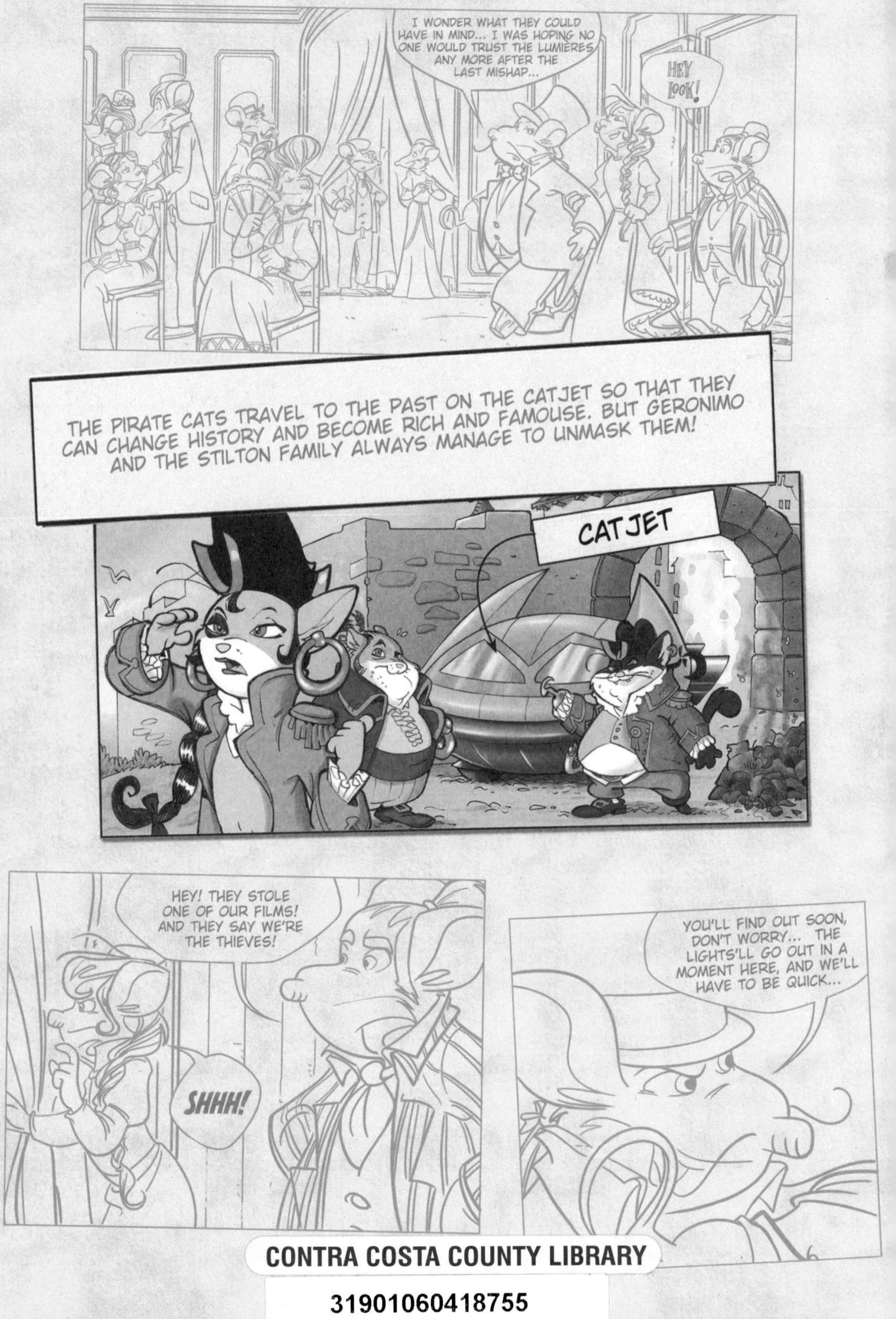
I WONDER WHAT THEY COULD HAVE IN MIND... I WAS HOPING NO ONE WOULD TRUST THE LUMIÈRES ANY MORE AFTER THE LAST MISHAP...
HEY LOOK!
THE PIRATE CATS TRAVEL TO THE PAST ON THE CATJET SO THAT THEY CAN CHANGE HISTORY AND BECOME RICH AND FAMOUSE. BUT GERONIMO AND THE STILTON FAMILY ALWAYS MANAGE TO UNMASK THEM!
CATJET
HEY! THEY STOLE ONE OF OUR FILMS! AND THEY SAY WE'RE THE THIEVES!
SHHH!
YOU'LL FIND OUT SOON, DON'T WORRY... THE LIGHTS'LL GO OUT IN A MOMENT HERE, AND WE'LL HAVE TO BE QUICK...